D0365846

*The Ghost of Brannock Hall*

Copyright © 1993 Ann Roede.

Published by:
Playground Book Publishing Company.

Cover Illustration by: Michael F. McCormick
©1993 Michael F. McCormick

Cover Design by:
    Harris Design Office
    742 Yorklyn Road
    Suite 325
    Hockessin, DE 19707

For more information, contact the publisher:
    Playground Books Publishing Company
    P.O. Box 3030
    Wilmington, DE 19804
    (302)655-4408

ISBN # 0-9638237-0-1

# CONTENTS

# ARRIVAL AT BRANNOCK HALL

"We're here."

Aunt Kate turned the car into the circular driveway. The old house lay in front of them, cold and dark in the fading winter afternoon. The branches of an enormous oak tree behind it were outlined bleakly against the gray sky, and the scene looked deserted and uninviting.

Fourteen-year-old Brad slumped in the back seat. It was worse than he expected, and he had to spend six months here! He glanced at his twin sister, Dru, but she gave him a warning frown and shook her head. He had not spoken a word all the way from the airport, and she was a little ashamed of him.

She began to chatter politely to Aunt Kate. "Brad and I can't wait to see Brannock Hall again, Aunt Kate. We don't really remember much about it, but it seems like we do. We're really looking forward to our visit with you while Mom and Dad are in South America. Aren't we Brad?" She jabbed him viciously with her elbow.

Suddenly he was sitting bolt upright looking at something out the back window. Lying in the corner of Aunt Kate's property, half hidden by a hedge of overgrown yews, was an old cemetery. What was a cemetery doing in Aunt Kate's front yard? The sun was setting behind it, and the twisted old yews were silhouetted in its red glow. Ropes of Spanish moss hanging from their branches swayed in the cold wind, and shadows thrown by the tall gravestones threw ugly pockets of darkness on the wet grass. The whole thing was surrounded by a black iron fence with long, sharp spikes. With an effort, Brad pulled his eyes away. He tried to concentrate on what Dru was saying, but something about that mysterious cemetery had frightened him.

Dru was leaning forward, peering eagerly at the old house. They knew all about it. The Brannock family heritage. Built by Colonel Justin Brannock in 1790, it was the most important piece of history in Brannock County, North Carolina. When they were small children, they had visited Aunt Kate, but it had been more than ten years since they had seen the old home, and most of their memories came from their father who had spent his vacations here when he was a boy. Brad sighed. The house looked older and smaller than he remembered. It was going to be a long visit!

Aunt Kate fitted the key into the heavy iron lock. "Welcome to Brannock Hall!"

She threw open the door and stepped aside to let them enter. Dru glanced at Brad and stifled a giggle. It was pitch black inside, and neither of them wanted to walk through the door into the cold darkness.

"Oh my," Aunt Kate exclaimed, "I forgot to leave on a light!"

Brad waited outside while Dru felt her way over to Aunt Kate and helped her locate a lamp, and in a few moments there was a pool of soft light on the wooden floor. Brad stepped inside and sighed with relief as Aunt Kate adjusted a thermostat on the wall. Somehow he hadn't expected central heating in this old mausoleum, and he was glad to hear the sound of the furnace kicking in. At least they wouldn't be shivering in front of an open fire the rest of the winter.

Brad and Dru spent the next few minutes

carrying packages and bags from the car and dumping them on the floor beside the front door. When they had emptied the last bag, Aunt Kate appeared at the top of the porch steps with her car keys in her hands.

"I'm going to move the car around back to the old stable. It will only take a few minutes."

They stood on the porch watching as she started the car and drove around the half circle, her wheels crunching in the loose gravel.

Brad broke the silence. "She's passing that spooky graveyard."

As she rounded the curve of the drive, her headlights shone on the trees surrounding the cemetery, and they could see the thick Spanish moss moving slightly in the wind.

"I don't remember that graveyard from my visits when I was a baby."

"Well, it looks like it's been there forever," said Dru.

"I think it's the weirdest place I've ever seen," Brad said in a low voice. "I wonder why the Brannock's put it so close to the house? You'd think they'd have known better. This place is supposed to be a perfect specimen of taste and charm."

"I don't know," said Dru. "I suppose after a while they got used to it. Aunt Kate doesn't seem to mind."

They followed her headlights with their eyes. Just beyond the cemetery, the drive branched off to an old stable in back of the house where Aunt Kate kept her car. For some reason, neither Brad nor Dru felt like going inside, and for what seemed like a long time they peered silently into the darkness which appeared to have swallowed Aunt Kate. A sharp wind had begun to blow, and they hunched slightly forward, hugging themselves against the chill. The silence was broken at last by the faint "chunk" of the car door, and almost immediately a small, bobbing prick of light appeared.

"Good!" exclaimed Brad in relief. "She's got a flashlight."

They began to bounce from one foot to the other to restore circulation. "Let's go inside and get warm," suggested Dru. "Aunt Kate's okay. She'll be here in a minute."

"You go on in. I like it out here," said Brad. "Besides," he added, "I'm enjoying the balmy Southern weather."

Dru looked at him with disgust. "Right!" she said sarcastically. "Stay out here if you want, but I'm going inside."

Brad stood on the porch lost in thought. Something was wrong. He felt restless and uneasy. So much had happened in the past few weeks that he and Dru had not had time to think. When the University had offered Dad a grant to join a team of archaeologists who were excavating a Mayan village, the whole family had been excited. Mom had taken a year's leave and wrangled a position with the expedition as chief cataloger, and they had all assumed that Brad and Dru, who were freshmen in high school, would go with the family to South America. It was a shock to learn from one of Dad's contacts that there was no school anywhere near the excavation site. Everything screeched to a halt! For an entire day their plans had seemed doomed; then Dad remembered Aunt Kate.

"It's the very thing!" Mom exclaimed. "You'll have a marvelous time at Brannock Hall! Why, it's almost as good as being in South America. Besides, Aunt Kate must be lonely living in that big house all by herself, and she'll love having you for a few months. It's a perfect solution!"

It had been a perfect solution for everybody but Brad. Even now he could hardly believe how easily Dru had given up. He had never seen an archaeological dig, but he had no romantic ideas about them. He knew from Dad that the work was hard and boring, but he hadn't cared. He pictured himself carefully brushing away the sand from a small mound and unearthing something. Even a broken pot would be exciting! He felt sure he could do without school for a few months.

He stood now on the porch peering uneasily out into the night. Somehow, he couldn't shake the feeling that they were all in some kind of danger. Something was wrong, and it wasn't that he didn't want to be here. He had felt this way ever since he glimpsed the graveyard for the first time.

His eyes searched the darkness for Aunt Kate. He could see the beam of her powerful flashlight, and now he could faintly hear the crunch of her feet in the gravel as she walked past the cemetery. She was shining her light on the path in front of her, and even from this distance, Brad could see the rocks the beam picked out of the darkness.

Suddenly she flicked the light directly into the cemetery, and Brad caught a momentary glimpse of a white figure lurking among the trees! It looked human, but it was pale and formless. He couldn't make out the features of its face which seemed to be shadowed by some kind of hood, but it was the eyes that frightened him! They glowed through the night like a cat's, caught in the headlights, and they were fixed on him!

Almost instantly, Aunt Kate's light flicked back down to the ground, leaving the cemetery in darkness again. Brad's breath caught in his throat and he gasped aloud. He could feel his heart pounding beneath his shirt. He leapt down the steps and stood poised, ready to run to Aunt Kate's aid. She was so close now that he could see her face in the reflected glow from the flashlight, but she was smiling and her voice sounded normal.

"What are you doing out here, Brad? You'll freeze to death without a coat." She spoke cheerfully.

Brad watched in amazement as she calmly walked toward him. Was it possible that she hadn't seen the thing in the cemetery? Surely she had! She had shone her light directly on it. He could still feel his heart pounding madly beneath his shirt, and watched in disbelief as she climbed the porch steps and clicked off the flashlight.

She shivered. "It's the coldest night since

Slowly Brad straightened up. His dark eyes seemed huge in his pale face, and his voice trembled when he spoke. "No," he said softly. "I don't think so," but he looked frightened and almost sick.

Aunt Kate climbed quickly up the steps and put one arm around his shoulders. She felt his clammy forehead with her other hand. "I expect you're just tired," she said. "It's been a long day."

Brad silently picked up his duffel bag and followed as she led the way up the steps. He ignored Dru's worried frown.

"Did your father tell you about the hole in the wall?" Aunt Kate asked as she opened the door to Brad's room.

They nodded. At some point in the old home's past, a square hole had been cut low in the wall between the two bedrooms at one end of the second floor hall, and had been covered on each side with a grill. No one knew why the hole had been cut.

"Your father and his cousins used to love that hole," said Aunt Kate. "I could hear them talking back and forth all night, but if you want more privacy, I can move one of you to another bedroom."

Before Dru could answer, Brad spoke.

"This will be fine, Aunt Kate. If Dru snores, I can bang on the grate."

"Me? I've never snored in my life!"

"I'll leave you alone and let you get settled," she said. "If you need anything, you can call me. My bedroom is at the other end of the hall."

As soon as she had closed the door, Dru turned to Brad. "What happened to you on the steps? You looked like you had seen a ghost!"

Brad stared at her blankly. "Nothing," he said.

Dru sighed and gave up. She knew that he would tell her when the time was right. There was no sense in trying to force it out of him.

They stood for a moment looking around the room. There was a large bed with four tall posts pushed against the right wall next to the hold. Beside it stood a small table with a lamp. A fireplace was set in the paneled wall opposite, and a single chest stood in the corner. Next to the window in the third wall was an oak wardrobe with two doors, and the floor was bare except for a square of faded carpet. Dru's room next door was almost exactly like Brad's and he thought they were bare and ugly. He glanced quickly at the ceiling, and opened his duffel bag.

"What are you doing?" Dru asked curiously.

Brad was fishing around inside. From the blue nylon case, he pulled a roll of string and his Swiss army knife. "I'm going to attach a string to that cord hanging from the ceiling light and tie it to my bed post." He pointed to a post at the head of his bed. "That way, I can pull it when I need light at night. It's easier than groping around in the dark for the switch on the table lamp."

"Good idea!" exclaimed Dru, instantly impressed. "Do you have enough string for mine?"

"Sure," said Brad. "There's plenty."

It took only a few minutes to tie the string to the bed posts, and Brad found himself suddenly exhausted. He stretched and yawned. "I'm going to bed."

Dru was standing quietly looking at the hole. "That's a weird hole," she said. "It's big enough for a person to crawl through."

Brad stopped in mid yawn. "Don't even think it!" he said. "There's nothing in this house but us!"

"I wasn't thinking anything. All I said was it's a big hole. I don't think a ghoulie is going to crawl through it and grab you. That's crazy!"

"That's what I said!" repeated Brad. "There's nothing in this house but us. Nothing!"

Dru looked at him strangely as she opened the door. "I'll see you in the morning, Brad. You need a good night's sleep."

## EXPLORATIONS

As usual Brad awoke easily, his senses alert. He lay quietly in the big four-poster bed and looked around the room. Sunlight streamed in the window. It threw a patch of brilliance over the bare floor and plain wooden furniture. Brad stretched comfortably and yawned. He was glad to see the sunlight. Already last night seemed unreal, and he had fallen asleep so quickly that he had no time to sort through what had happened. He lay still now, lost in thought.

First, there was the uncanny feeling when they had driven into the yard and he had seen the cemetery. That one was easy, he thought. Nerves. The cemetery was spooky. Twisted trees with veils of Spanish moss, the black iron fence, broken gravestones - it looked like a scene from a horror movie. It was perfect!

The figure he had seen in the graveyard was harder. Last night it terrified him, but in the morning sunlight he could be more objective. Maybe it was some sort of scarecrow, he thought. For all he knew it was customary for people down here to put a weird figure in their cemeteries - some sort of voodoo protection, maybe. He'd have to check it out in the daylight.

What was really bothering him was what happened on the stairs. Both he and Dru, whose common sense was usually reliable, had both sensed real danger in the darkness, but lying here in the bright morning, he could dismiss that too. Nerves again. Okay, but what about the voice he had heard coming to him from that dark hole above the landing? That was not so easy to explain. "Rose," he thought it said. He was almost sure of it. What a strange word to hear coming from the blackness above him! Maybe it was "nose" or "hose." None of them made any sense, and he didn't like any of this. For just a moment he wished Aaron's jokes about the insane relative in the attic were true. Any explanation, no matter how strange, would be welcome.

Idly he glanced around the room. Suddenly his eyes were caught by the string above his bed. It was cut. Dru! He'd just replace it and say nothing about it. He grinned when he thought of her reaction. She wouldn't be able to stand it! He jumped out of bed, and in a minute another string was attached from the cord to the bed post. He grabbed his jeans from the chair where he had thrown them and began pulling them on.

"Brad," came Dru's voice from the hole. "Are you awake?"

"Yes," he answered. "Hours ago. I've already had breakfast and jogged six miles."

"Sure!" said Dru. There was a short silence. "Things look different in the daytime, don't they?"

Brad glanced around the room in surprise. "Not especially," he said. "Why?"

"I don't know. It just all looks better in the daylight."

"I guess so," he said. "Hurry up, Dru! I want to look around."

He clattered down the steps and out the front door, followed more quietly by Dru. They stopped on the porch and stood looking toward the cemetery. He was right! It did look spooky, but nothing could actually be that frightening in broad daylight.

Dru was still puzzled. "Why did they put

it so close to the house?" she wondered aloud.

Aunt Kate spoke from the door behind them. "You've noticed the old graveyard. I'm so used to it, I forget how strange it must look. When they were excavating in 1790, the workmen discovered an Indian burial ground. It was too late to save most of the graves, but the Colonel was able to protect this section. It actually became a tourist attraction, and people came from miles around to see it."

"But, Aunt Kate, there are tall gravestones in there. Surely they weren't put there by the Indians."

"No, the Indians didn't use gravestones. They were put there by the family. They used the plot for their house servants when they died. The Brannocks themselves had a plot on the hill behind the house, but when most of the property was sold in the 1920's, the family remains were moved to the new county cemetery."

She turned to go back inside. "I'll call you for breakfast in a little while."

Brad stood looking at the cemetery. "Indians!" he thought in relief. Maybe that would explain the figure he had seen last night. Old Justin had probably found a totem pole somewhere and stuck it in among the burial mounds. Probably attracted ancient tourists like flies!

"Come on!" Dru said. "Let's get a closer look."

They walked down the driveway toward the cemetery. It was still cold, but the mid-morning sun was bright, and Brad had regained his confidence. The events of the night before might almost have been a bad dream. As they walked, he tried to tell Dru about the figure he had seen in the cemetery, and the fright it had given him. In the daylight it sounded ridiculous, even to him.

"But, Brad, if Aunt Kate didn't see it, it must not have been anything. Maybe you saw some Spanish moss. It twists around and takes strange shapes."

"It had eyes!" exclaimed Brad in disgust. "Spanish moss doesn't have eyes!"

"Your imagination was playing tricks on you. You surely don't think some restless Indian spirit is patrolling the burial grounds."

"No, I guess not," Brad grinned. "It does seem silly this morning, but it was different last night."

"So that's why you looked so funny when you followed Aunt Kate inside! You looked like you'd seen a ghost - if you'll pardon the expression."

"Very funny!" said Brad.

They reached the cemetery and stood looking through the fence. The plot was bigger than it looked from the house. There were fifteen or twenty tall grave markers in front - some of them broken in half. The broken pieces lay among the weeds in an untidy mess. There were no markers in the back, but the ground appeared to be softly mounded in several places.

"It looks like the Indian graves are in back. They must be buried in those mounds. These must be the servants' gravestones up here in front. I don't see anything that looks like a totem pole. Can you remember where you saw the figure, Brad?"

"Aunt Kate was walking past the cemetery and reached these trees right here in front. She flashed her light on that tree right there. The figure was standing beside it and a little bit behind it. Aunt Kate should have seen it. It wasn't hiding."

"Well, that lets the Indians out, anyway," said Dru. "The figure you saw was standing up front where the servants' graves are."

She hesitated, her mind on something else. "Brad, I can read the date on that stone," she said, pointing to the one nearest the gate. "It says, '1815-1855.' That was before the Civil War."

"That's right," said Brad, glad to change the subject.

"Well, then why does Aunt Kate call the people buried here 'servants?' They must have been slaves."

"I noticed that, too," said Brad. "You'd think she'd know the difference. After all, she taught history at Brannock High School for thirty-five years."

"Maybe," Dru said, "she hates to admit there was ever any blemish on the record of her famous family. You know, now that I think about it, most of what's written by the historical society is about the original Colonel Brannock. There's not much information about the history of the house during the Civil War except Robert, Justin's son, was killed in a skirmish near Kinston. Maybe Aunt Kate knows something she doesn't want us to know."

"I don't know," said Brad, losing interest. "Let's go see what's behind the house."

"Okay," said Dru. "There's obviously nothing of interest in the cemetery."

"There was last night!" said Brad, suddenly

angry and ready to argue.

"Fine," said Dru. "Maybe it was a raccoon on a stump, or something."

Brad nodded. He felt a little better. "Might have been. It makes more sense than anything else we've come up with."

And it really did, he thought, feeling slightly embarrassed. The eyes he had seen peering at him through the darkness could have been raccoon eyes reflecting the light from Aunt Kate's flashlight.

He followed Dru around the cemetery to the stable. Brannock Hall had an unusual history for an old house. It had remained in one family ever since it was built in 1790, and it still held its original furniture, which were priceless antiques now. In the 1800's, the Brannock who owned it decided to live in town. The furniture was covered with sheets, and wooden planks were nailed over the doors and windows. Nobody lived there again until thirty years ago when Aunt Kate's widowed mother inherited Brannock Hall, and to everyone's surprise opened the house and moved in.

It wasn't long before the people in the county became aware of the historical value of the old place, but they wanted Aunt Kate and her mother to treat it like a museum. Every time they added a modern convenience, such as electricity, people like Ida Lou Duncan, president of the Brannock County Historical Society, were sure to come nosing around. She felt that, "Kate had absolutely no right to destroy the historical authenticity of the jewel of the county!" The very mention of Ida Lou threw Aunt Kate into a fit.

They passed the stable, which now held Aunt Kate's car, and walked around to a building which lay directly behind the main house.

"Hey!" exclaimed Dru. "I remember this building. It's the old kitchen."

"How can you remember that, Dru? We were only four the last time we were here."

"But I do remember! I was confused because I couldn't understand why there was a kitchen in the house with a refrigerator and a stove, and another kitchen in the back yard with nothing but a fireplace which no one ever used."

Brad laughed. "Yeah, it did seem strange that one house had two kitchens. We didn't know that in the old days they built their kitchens in the back yard so if they caught on fire, they wouldn't burn the main house."

Dru laughed. "Aunt Kate's friend, Ida Lou,

probably thinks she should still be cooking out here over an open fire."

She stood on her toes and peered inside a grimy window. She could make out a jumble of dusty objects, partly obscured by gray sheets of cobwebs. Brad began to scrape at one of the windows while Dru walked around the building to the front. A white picket fence surrounded the entrance and formed a small garden.

The remains of a brick walk led from the old kitchen to the back porch of Brannock Hall. It was pitted now, and buckled in places, and a thick hedge of English boxwood ran along either side. Dru could almost picture a dark woman in a long skirt, a bright turban wrapped around her head, hurriedly carrying a smoking platter to the house before it cooled.

Brad joined her and stood looking at the old kitchen.

"It looks ..." He struggled for a word to describe it. "Comfortable," he decided.

Dru laughed. "You like anything that deals with food - past or present. You never met a kitchen you didn't like!"

Brad laughed. He glanced around the yard and tried to visualize where the other farm buildings might have stood. There had been an overseer's house he knew from reading the brochures, and there must have been a smokehouse and a spring house. Somewhere there had been slave quarters. None of them remained.

"Let's go in," Dru said, suddenly hungry. "Maybe Aunt Kate has breakfast ready. She wants us to unpack this morning, and this afternoon she's going to take us to the high school to enroll. I heard her calling somebody named David to make plans."

The morning passed quickly, but soon after lunch Brad disappeared. After a short search Dru found him in front of the TV. "Come on," she said. "Aunt Kate is waiting for us in the car."

"You go," Brad answered. "I want to finish watching this show."

"Oh, no you don't! You've got to come, too. You're still in a bad mood, but you know you've got to do this. Let's just get it over with."

"I don't want to change my clothes. You can enroll for both of us."

"You look fine, Brad. It's the weekend. Nobody, except David, is there anyhow. I'm not enrolling for you. You've got to do it yourself!"

Brad groaned and got up. He flopped into the back seat, and sat staring at his hands. Dru gave him a disgusted look, and looked with interest out the window. The flat, sandy land was different from the countryside around their home in northern Delaware. They rode in silence for a few miles.

"Hey, Brad!" Dru whispered in a low voice. "That speed limit sign we just passed said 35 mph."

Brad looked up in surprise. "No way! The speed limit is always 55 on these country roads."

"I don't care," insisted Dru. "that small, white sign back there said 35 mph! I'm sure of it!"

Brad looked anxiously at Aunt Kate who was sitting calmly in the driver's seat. The needle of the speedometer was resting squarely on 55. The road ran straight and black through fields of tobacco. The land was flat and empty. There seemed no reason why the speed limit should change. He relaxed.

Suddenly Dru, who had been looking out the back window stiffened. "Oh, no!" she groaned under her breath. She turned around and slipped down in her seat. She covered her eyes with her hands.

Brad jerked around in time to see a brown and white sedan pulling out from behind a billboard. As he watched, a muscular arm emerged from the car window and clamped a magnetic flashing light to the roof. A siren blasted a warning shot.

"Aunt Kate! You'd better pull over!"

"Oh, my!" exclaimed Aunt Kate. She looked flustered, and swerved so quickly that her tires caught in the soft sand along the edge of the road. The car rocked dangerously before she brought it under control.

Brad and Dru looked out the back window as the car pulled up behind them. The door opened and a large man got out. He was wearing a wide brimmed hat and what looked like tan jodhpurs. His polished boots crunched threateningly in the loose gravel as he approached Aunt Kate's car.

"Oh, no!" hissed Brad. "It's one of those Southern sheriffs! We're road kill!"

The deputy rested both elbows on Aunt Kate's window and leaned over to look inside. His jaws worked slowly over a piece of gum, and what Brad could see of his neck under the shadow of his hat looked thicker than his head. He was wearing aviator sunglasses. Brad shot an anxious glance at Aunt Kate. She suddenly seemed very small and gray.

He jumped when she spoke. "Well! If it isn't Randy Travers!"

The transformation was amazing! The deputy jumped upright so swiftly he banged his head on the window frame. He snatched his hat from his head, and stood looking sheepishly at her.

Dru shot a surprised look at Brad.

"Randy Travers!" Aunt Kate repeated in delight. "The high school was never the same after you graduated. How have you been?"

"Fine, Miss Kate," he answered, grinning foolishly. Dru noticed that he was turning his hat nervously in his hands.

"Well, I must say, you turned out better than I expected," laughed Aunt Kate, "but I always knew you'd end up in the hands of the law!"

The deputy grinned politely at the old joke and adjusted his glasses. He was obviously embarrassed.

"Well, it's mighty good to see you again, Miss Kate," he said sincerely. "You always were my favorite teacher." He gave the car a friendly slap with his hand as he backed hastily away. "Y'all take care now," he said.

"Randolph Eugene Travers!" snapped Aunt

Kate. "Was I or was I not exceeding the posted speed limit?"

"Yes m'am," he answered.

"Well, then you'd better write me out a ticket!"

Brad and Dru watched as he obediently moistened a pencil with the tip of his tongue and wrote something on a pad. He tore the slip from the pad and handed it anxiously to Aunt Kate as though he expected her to check it for spelling errors. When she had signed it, he tipped his hat and returned to his car. The last Brad saw of his was a respectful wave of his hand as he executed a neat U-turn and headed back toward town. He passed the billboard without stopping.

Aunt Kate folded the pink slip and stuck it carefully in a pocket of her purse. "Well!" she said briskly. "It's always nice to see one of my students again, though Randy Travers ought to know better. He should be ashamed of himself. One thing you could always count on him for was fair play."

Dru was puzzled. "It's his job to give tickets to speeders."

"Of course it is, but it's not his job to establish an illegal speed trap. The sheriff is famous for doing this sort of thing, but now he's got to deal with me!" She snapped her pocketbook shut with a determined pop.

Brad looked at Dru and raised his eyebrows. Aunt Kate was someone to reckon with in Brannock County!

"The high school is not much further now," she said, starting the engine. "It's only fifteen minutes or so from Brannock Hall, but Mrs. Pollock says it takes about thirty minutes on the school bus. Sarah is visiting her grandparents in Myrtle Beach this week, but she'll come by the house Monday morning and walk with you to the bus stop."

"Great!" said Dru happily. She was eager to meet Sarah Pollock. According to Aunt Kate, she was the only other fourteen-year-old girl in the neighborhood.

Brad was not paying attention to the conversation. He was looking out the window, hoping to catch sight of the high school. It was probably old he thought, like Brannock Hall, but they might have a computer somewhere. Surely something around here was made after 1790!

He was surprised when Aunt Kate turned through two white posts into a drive which lead through a rolling green field. Long, low, white brick buildings lay in front of them. It took a moment for him to realize that these were school buildings. It was all very new and modern. There were glass walls with laboratories behind them, and on one of the eastern corners, he could see the curving wall of a greenhouse.

"Wow!" he said.

"Is this it?" exclaimed Dru.

"Yes," said Aunt Kate with pride. "Brand new two years ago."

"But I thought you taught at the high school," Dru said in confusion.

"I did," answered Aunt Kate, "before it was moved. Now, let's go in and see if David is here."

"David" turned out to be Mr. Anderson, the high school principal and another one of Aunt Kate's former students. He walked with them down the polished corridors, unlocking door after door as he and Aunt Kate talked enthusiastically. Dru noticed a computer lab connected to the media center, but decided not to comment on it. She glimpsed the quick grin on Brad's face, though.

On the way home, Brad and Dru chatted excitedly, their spirits high. Things were definitely looking up, Brad decided. Before reaching Brannock Hall, they stopped at the grocery store and helped Aunt Kate fill a grocery basket. The cashier was one of Aunt Kate's students. So was the store manager. Both of them helped carry her grocery bags out to the car.

The sky was graying in the winter afternoon as they pulled into the driveway in front of Brannock Hall. Aunt Kate turned off beyond the cemetery and circled around to the back of the house where they could unload the groceries near the kitchen. Brad took the house key and ran up the porch steps, two at a time. The key turned easily in the lock and he heard the tumblers click smoothly. He gave the door a slight shove, but it wouldn't open. Surprised, he shoved it again - harder. This time, it moved slightly at the top, but remained stuck tight at the bottom, as if someone inside had their foot jammed against the base of the door!

Brad's good humor evaporated. He felt the hairs on the back of his neck rise, and the chill of the bleak afternoon seemed to penetrate his jacket. He backed away from the door and bolted down the steps. The sight of Aunt Kate's sensible face calmed him slightly, and he picked up two grocery bags and followed her up the steps. She was chatting to

Dru over her shoulder and did not pause as she approached the door. Brad held his breath as she grasped the doorknob. The door opened easily and Aunt Kate stepped briskly inside. Dru followed her, still laughing about something.

Brad stepped slowly over the threshold, his eyes darting fearfully around the room. Aunt Kate set her grocery bags on the counter and looked about her in satisfaction. She had formed the modern kitchen from two old store rooms and a small, dark scullery. It was new and modern, and she was proud of it.

"I declare, it's always good to get home! If you'll put the groceries away for me, I'll start dinner."

"Come on, Brad!" said Dru. "Quit standing there looking dumb! You put the canned stuff in the pantry, and I'll work on the stuff that goes in the refrigerator."

Brad picked up a bag of groceries and began placing the contents in the pantry. "Stop being so foolish," he told himself. "The door was stuck. That's all."

By the time they finished putting the groceries away, the smell of the hamburgers Aunt Kate was cooking filled the kitchen. Dru was hungry and was glad when they finally sat down at the table. She and Aunt Kate chatted happily during the meal, but Brad remained unusually quiet.

After they had finished, Aunt Kate said, "Now, let's clean up the kitchen. I have some work I need to do tonight."

"Me, too," said Dru. "I want to make sure everything is ready for school Monday."

"What do you plan to do, Brad?" Aunt Kate asked suddenly.

Brad was taken by surprise. "Why don't we all do something together?" he suggested.

"Like what?" asked Dru.

"I don't know." He hesitated. "Maybe we could watch TV or something."

"There's nothing good on. I've already checked," said Dru.

"Well, maybe we could do something else," said Brad.

"Like what?" Dru was curious.

"Like read a book or something."

"I do plan to read a book," said Dru in surprise, "but I don't want to do it with you watching!"

Aunt Kate looked at him inquiringly through her bifocals.

"I - I meant...all in the same room."

"Are you nuts?" Dru laughed as she pushed

her chair away from the table. She walked over to the sink and began scraping the dishes. She was in a hurry to finish.

Brad sighed. It was going to be a long evening. He knew he would spend it running up and down the steps checking on Dru and Aunt Kate.

There was something in the house!

# PLANS

"Mercy!" exclaimed Aunt Kate. She looked uneasily at the girl who opened the back door and entered the kitchen. Her long, dark hair hung in a thick, curly mass down her back. The bangs in front waved softly around her face, and the hair on the sides had been pulled straight up from her face and gathered on top with a red clamp. She was wearing jeans which were faded to a whitish color with only traces of the original blue. There were jagged holes in the knees, and a back pocket hung loose and torn. In addition, she was wearing what appeared to be one of her father's shirts. It billowed around her slender frame like an enormous bag.

"Why, it's Sarah Pollock!" exclaimed Aunt Kate in some distress.

Sarah greeted Dru and Brad cheerfully.

"Hurry up! We'll walk to the bus stop together, but we can't be late. The bus driver sometimes comes a few minutes early, and she never waits!"

Brad choked down the rest of his biscuit and grabbed his book bag. Dru jumped up and ran toward the stairs, calling over her shoulder, "I'll be down in a minute!"

"Hello, Miss Kate," Sarah said politely, turning toward her a pair of startlingly blue eyes framed in long, dark lashes. "Mom says to tell you she'll be a few minutes late to the meeting this afternoon. She has to pick up the car at the garage and stop by the library. She says to make sure you give her plenty of time for her report. She's been digging around in the county archives all week."

Aunt Kate was relieved to hear this matter-of-fact account from Sarah. All seemed normal at the Pollock house. For just a minute her eyes lingered on the holes in Sarah's jeans. "Oh, well," she thought.

Dru came running down the back steps into the cheerful kitchen. Her shining blond hair bounced and her green eyes sparkled. She was pleased with her new friend. For a second her eyes rested enviously on Sarah's designer jeans with the pre-torn knees. Mom would never allow her to buy a pair - too expensive!

Brad, who also appeared to be pleased with Sarah, hitched his book bag on his left shoulder and left the kitchen with the two girls. Aunt Kate noticed that he held the door open for them. Dru noticed too, and raised her eyebrows at him behind Sarah's back, but Brad grinned and flashed a thumbs-up sign at Aunt Kate before the door banged shut behind him.

She walked to the front parlor and watched them from the window as they walked together down the drive. Sarah was in the middle and Dru and Brad were on either side. The three were laughing and talking as though they were old friends. She watched them until they turned the corner onto the street and the cemetery hid them from view.

When she turned away, there was a smile on her face. It was nice having young people in the house again. It had been a long time. She was a little worried about the summer vacation, though. In just a few months, school would be out, and she knew she'd have to find something to occupy their time. She had been turning a plan over in her mind, and now that she had spent a few days with the twins, she felt sure it would work.

The old kitchen in the back yard was crammed with junk. In all the years she had lived at Brannock Hall, she had seldom been inside it, but she had a pretty shrewd idea of the value of the junk. People in this part of the state were eager for anything from Brannock Hall, and even the broken things would probably bring a good price. If Brad and Dru would help her clean out the kitchen, they could sell whatever she didn't want and share the profits.

She needed to work out the details, but it was a good plan. And the best thing about it was that Ida Lou would have a perfect fit! It would drive her crazy that "Kate was actually selling those irreplaceable antiques!" She smiled grimly as she turned to the sink.

"Aunt Kate!" shouted Brad that afternoon, as he clattered inside the back door and threw his books on the kitchen table. "You remember that booklet Mr. Anderson gave us that listed the school activities? Well, I went to see the faculty newspaper advisor, and she hired me as a photographer! They have a great system here. She's had one of the hall storage closets on the second floor converted into a darkroom, and the student photographers can develop their own prints. She'll buy what the newspaper can use from us and we can sell the rest to the other students."

Sarah and Dru followed Brad into the kitchen and stood looking at him in amusement. He was carried away by his excitement, and as he talked he kept running his hands through the dark shock of hair which fell over his forehead. Dru was used to his sudden enthusiasms, but Sarah was intrigued. She watched as he turned suddenly and clattered up the steps to get his camera.

"Man!" he exclaimed in disgust as he entered his room. His eyes went to the cord tied to the ceiling light. Broken again! This was the third time this week, and it was becoming irritating. He had to hand it to Dru, though. She usually got tired of a practical joke, but this time she was becoming obnoxious.

He grabbed his camera equipment and ran back downstairs. The girls watched as he attached the camera to a tripod and set it on automatic. He listened to the warning "beep-beep" as he raced back to the table and plopped down between them. He over-balanced, and the shutter clicked just as he fell to the floor, legs flailing wildly. Dru doubled up with laughter, while Sarah looked on in amusement. It was times like this that she missed not having a brother or sister.

While Brad reset the camera, Dru called to Aunt Kate. "Come sit between us! Brad can stand up. He can probably manage that since it doesn't require a lot of coordination."

As Aunt Kate settled herself between the two girls, she watched with interest while Brad moved the tripod and adjusted the camera for a close-up. She had no idea he was so good.

"How would you like to take some shots of Brannock Hall?" she suggested. "If you could get some good ones, I believe you could sell them to the historical society."

"Great!" said Brad. "I need a cash infusion, and I have almost a whole roll of film left."

He opened the kitchen door and looked at the gray January sky. The clear winter light sharpened the outline of the grass and bare trees.

"Perfect!" he exclaimed. "I can start now. This is the best kind of light to photograph a building - sharp but without direct sunlight. I'll have to hurry. It gets dark quickly."

Dru began to cram his equipment into his bag, but she was not too busy to notice how pleased Brad was when Sarah picked up his tripod and followed them outside. She sighed. Although she had been interested in Sarah right from the beginning, Brad had seemed completely uninterested. Yet in the few short days since he met her in the kitchen that morning, he had managed to learn that she was a beauty! Brad somehow discovered these things. It was like osmosis. The presence of an attractive girl seemed to enter his consciousness through some sort of capillary action.

Dru also knew through long experience Brad's effect on her friends. His quick, athletic body and dark brown eyes seemed irresistible, and she had learned to be suspicious of girls who played up to her so they could make time with Brad. Fortunately, Brad usually saw through those tactics, and none of his relationships lasted long; but Sarah seemed different. She was interested in Brad, but she wasn't falling all over him. Dru had a feeling Brad might have to work for this one!

For the next hour they were almost too busy to talk. Brad issued orders, and Dru and Sarah worked efficiently. All of them were aware of the quickly fading light. Sarah seemed interested in what they were doing, and beyond asking several questions, was happy to work quietly with them. Dru liked her more and more. She had never before seen a girl as beautiful as Sarah who wasn't happy unless she was the center of attention. She watched as Sarah quickly fastened the camera to the tripod and stepped back to let Brad make the final adjustments.

"There!" Brad exclaimed as he snapped the shutter and began unfastening the camera almost simultaneously. "This is the last shot I need from this angle, but it might be nice to get a couple of long distance views from the back. You two run ahead and find a good angle. I'll grab this stuff and follow."

Dru glanced apprehensively at the pale sun which was sinking slowly toward the horizon, and ran quickly around the house. She was a better runner than Sarah, and easily outdistanced her. As she ran, she glanced over her shoulder to gauge the best angle for Brad's shot. Suddenly she stumbled and landed heavily on her stomach. She lay stunned for a moment, trying to catch her breath.

She heard Sarah call anxiously, "Dru! Dru! Are you okay?"

Dru sat up shakily and looked around. She found she was sitting in a weed covered patch about twelve feet square. It was indented in the ground like a shallow pit, and she realized she had fallen over its edge.

As she heard Sarah approaching, she got to her feet with a shaky smile, but the smile froze on her lips when she glimpsed Sarah's face. She had stopped a few feet away, and there was an odd look in her eyes which seemed to be focused on something far away. To Dru's surprise, she suddenly whirled around and headed swiftly back.

"Sarah!" Dru called, catching up with her. Sarah's face was pale and she was breathing hard.

Sarah looked at her in embarrassment. "I'm sorry," she apologized. "It's just that this spot gives me the creeps! When I was little, I would never play out here with the other children because I was so afraid!"

Dru looked around her curiously. The yard looked like hundreds of others she had seen. The winter stubble was rough under her feet, but there was nothing strange about that. A few oak trees were scattered here and there, and a couple of dogwoods, but there was nothing else in it. Nothing to be afraid of!

"What is it, Sarah?" she asked curiously. "What's frightening you?"

"It's the pit!" Sarah explained.

Dru glanced back over her shoulder. "What about it?" she asked, confused.

"A long time ago it was used for cock fighting. Men used to throw roosters into the pit
and watch them fight and they took bets on
which one would kill the other first. They were
not allowed to stop fighting until one of them
had pecked and gouged the other to death.
Even the one that survived would eventually
be killed because he had to keep on fighting
other cocks. It was bloody and cruel!"

"That's terrible!" Dru agreed. "Did you ever
see one of the fights?"

"Oh, no!" Sarah exclaimed. "It's against the
law now. I don't think that pit has been used
since before the Civil War."

Dru was puzzled. "How do you know
about the cock fights, then?"

"Oh, everybody around here knows about
them. Besides, I was born in Brannock County
and have lived near Brannock Hall all my life.
We even study it in school. Miss Kate lets
classes come out here on field trips."

The girls stood silently for a moment. Sarah spoke suddenly. "I know I'm sounding
crazy, but I get a funny feeling when I'm out
here, almost like deja vu, as though something
happened to me once that I can't remember,
but know must have been horrible!"

Dru looked at her thoughtfully. She was

sounding crazy! Worse, she was sounding a little like a fake. Was this some sort of ploy to prove how sensitive she was in order to impress Brad?

Sarah suddenly linked her arm through Dru's and began walking toward the house. She didn't speak again, but Dru noticed there was tight, white line around her mouth, and her arm was trembling. She was suddenly ashamed of her suspicions. Sarah had been afraid of something!

Just then Brad came struggling around the corner with his arms full of camera equipment. "Come on!" Dru called to him. "It's no good back here! Let's take a picture of the cemetery while the sun is setting."

Sarah gave her a grateful look. "Yeah!" she called. "We'll have to hurry before the spooks come out!"

"Hey!" shouted Brad as the girls ran around the stable. "Grab some of this stuff, will you!" But he stood watching them for a moment. Sarah was beautiful - no doubt about that - but, he had to admit, so was Dru. Her shining blond hair was cut short on the sides and in front, but behind it was slightly longer, and swirled when she turned her head. Other girls had tried to copy the style, but their hair usually turned out looking limp or crooked. She was very slender, and her green eyes sometimes seemed too big for her face, but her fragile appearance was deceiving. She had been a member of the varsity tennis team, and was on her way to becoming the top-seated woman player before their move to North Carolina.

As he stood between the two girls, adjusting the camera to catch the best angle of the old cemetery while the late afternoon shadows began to fall, he suddenly realized that he was no longer afraid. How different from the first time he had seen the old graveyard a week ago! "It must have been the Spanish moss," he thought. There was nothing frightening about it now. He felt a sense of relief. For the first time since arriving at Brannock Hall, he was completely relaxed. He caught Sarah's eye and grinned happily at her. His year with Aunt Kate was shaping up to be A-OK, after all!

## NIGHT FRIGHT

Brad was on a boat and it was rocking violently up and down. As it hit the crest of the wave, it bounced sharply and threw his body around. He could hear the loud slap, slap of the boat's bottom as it smacked against the water.

He jerked awake abruptly. It was his bed! The heavy four-poster was jerking violently up and down. The room was pitch black and unbearably cold. Was it an earthquake? He groped for the cord above his head, his arms flailing wildly. He couldn't find it!

As he stared madly into the darkness, his eyes began to pick up a faint gleam from the opposite end of the bed. He stared at it with horror! The gleam gradually congealed into a figure which was wearing what appeared to be a white, hooded robe. Inside the hood, where the face should be, was only darkness: except the eyes! They were the same eyes he had seen staring at him from the figure in the cemetery that first night, and he was unable to tear his own eyes away. In the darkness, the eyes of the figure glowed at him like small, evil neon lights.

He felt the corner of the bed drop with a heavy bang. The figure, eyes still riveted to his, lifted one arm and beckoned to him. Then it glided through the door, which Brad knew was closed. The whole incident had lasted only a few seconds, but it had seemed like a lifetime.

Brad was stiff with fright! He was literally unable to move. The faint gleam which the figure had produced had gradually faded leaving the room in darkness. His heart was pounding so loudly that his chest was jerking, and the blood was surging through his skull with such force that he could feel the power behind his ear drums. He was dizzy with terror but unable to cry out or make a sound.

He was only dimly aware of Aunt Kate's hurried footsteps on the stairs. Somewhere, he could hear Dru's voice crying his name. As Aunt Kate entered his room with her flashlight, he was seized with a fit of nausea. Later, he knew it was a simple reflex action which forced his legs out of bed and into the bathroom. He knelt and retched into the toilet and spent several minutes splashing soothing hot water onto his face.

His panic slowly subsided. He had to regain control! He became aware that Aunt Kate and Dru were talking worriedly outside in the hall. He forced himself to open the door, and stood swaying slightly, still speechless, his face white and drawn.

Aunt Kate took charge immediately. "Poor child!" she said. "Why, you've been taken ill." She took his arm and steadied him as she led him back to his bed. She tucked the blankets tightly around his trembling legs and fluffed his pillow. Brad could only lie quietly and watch her.

"Oh, my!" she clucked in irritation. "This string is broken again. Turn on the table lamp, Dru. We need light in here."

Dru silently switched on the lamp, and stood uncertainly, her eyes fixed on Brad. "Now," said Aunt Kate, "I'll just run downstairs and fix us a nice cup of hot tea. I'll get some medicine, too. You'll soon feel better." She headed purposefully toward the door.

"Aunt Kate!" Brad forced himself to speak through his chattering teeth. "Don't go downstairs alone!"

"Nonsense!" said Aunt Kate. "I'll be right back. Dru, you stay with him a few minutes."

He watched helplessly as she left the room. Dru stood with her eyes fixed anxiously on Brad. "Are you okay, Brad? What happened? What was that horrible bumping and clattering? I kept screaming for you, but you wouldn't answer."

Brad lay back weakly against the pillow. "It was a ghost, Dru. It was jerking the bed around."

To his surprise, Dru continued to look at him calmly. "I thought so, Brad. Funny things have been happening ever since we arrived. Your ghost in the cemetery was strange enough, but this afternoon Sarah sensed something strange, too; and Sarah seems pretty level headed. When I heard the noises tonight, I was terrified something was hurting you, but it was so dark I couldn't see to get to you. You've got to quit cutting my light cord!"

"Me!" exclaimed Brad, with a trace of his old energy. "I haven't been cutting your cord, you've been cutting mine!"

They stood staring at each other in amazement, then Dru managed a weak laugh. She jumped on Brad's bed, and tucked her feet under her. "At least it's got a sense of humor!"

She was thoughtful for a few seconds. "I wonder what Aunt Kate knows about it. It must have been around here for years. I'm surprised she's never mentioned it. She doesn't seem to be afraid of it."

They could hear the "clink" of dishes as Aunt Kate climbed the stairs. Dru ran to help her, and they entered the room a few seconds later carrying a tray with three mugs of steaming tea and a bottle of pink medicine. Aunt Kate placed the chair near the bed, and sat comfortably down. She handed each of them a mug. They looked expectantly at her as they sipped the hot liquid.

"Well," she said matter-of-factly. "You look a little better already. As soon as you finish your tea, I'll give you a dose of medicine. I'll check on you during the night. If you don't feel better by morning, you may have to miss a day at school."

Brad and Dru exchanged a look of disbelief. "Aunt Kate," said Dru slowly, choosing her words carefully, "didn't you hear some strange noises coming from Brad's room?"

"Of course I did," she answered. "I heard you calling. I came just as fast as I could. Now," she said as she placed her empty mug on the tray and picked up the pink bottle, "three tablespoons should be enough."

Brad was too weak to object, and opened his mouth obediently with the thought that nothing else could be as bad as what he had already gone through that night. Surprisingly, the pink medicine was so disgusting, it began to revive him.

Aunt Kate set the bottle on the table. "I'll say goodnight, now. Be sure and call me if you feel sick again." She placed her cool hand against Brad's hot forehead before she left the room.

Brad and Dru sat in silence for a few minutes, both lost in thought. Dru broke the silence. "She doesn't see or hear anything! She has no idea what's going on in her own house! I wonder what's wrong with her!"

Brad hesitated. "I don't think there's anything wrong with her," he said thoughtfully. "I've been wondering about it for days, and I think I've figured out why she doesn't see or hear the things I do. I think her mind is closed to any suggestion that there are some things in this world that don't make logical sense.

You know how she is. She can't imagine that spirits might exist in a dimension outside her common sense world, and it would never occur to her that a ghost lives in her house! If we told her one did, she wouldn't believe us. Not even our ghost can break through that kind of certainty. It probably gives her a sort of protection. She doesn't see it, smell it, sense it, or believe in it; so, it can't hurt her because it can't get through to her." Brad gave a short laugh. "It probably gave up in disgust a long time ago, and is looking for somebody else to torment. I just wish it hadn't chosen me!"

Dru was thoughtful for a few minutes, turning over Brad's theory in her mind. "But, Brad, does that mean your mind is somehow more evil than Aunt Kate's!"

"I can't exactly explain it, Dru, but I don't think so. It's just that Aunt Kate has developed into a certain kind of person. We know it, and somehow the ghost knows it, too. It may even be that my mind is more perceptive than hers, but the important thing is that we never tell her anything about the ghost. We mustn't ever give her any reason to suspect there's a crack in her common sense world. I think it might be dangerous to open her mind to that possibility. As long as she doesn't believe in it, it doesn't exist for her, and it can't hurt her because something that doesn't exist isn't dangerous."

He was thoughtful for a moment. "In all fairness, it has never actually tried to hurt us, either. In fact, now that I think about it, I believe it may have been asking for help tonight. It seemed to be calling to me."

Dru shuddered, but she answered with a brief laugh. "Yeah, ghosts do that in stories. They beckon people to follow them, then they fade away into graveyards where there's been a murder or something ..."

Her voice trailed off and she looked with horror at Brad who was staring wide-eyed back at her.

"No-o-o," breathed Dru softly. "It can't be!"

"It was in the old cemetery that first night, and it did ask me to follow it tonight," Brad said thoughtfully. "maybe it's time we checked out the cemetery," he added.

Dru's face turned white and she grabbed Brad's hands. "Bradley Justin Brannock," she said urgently. "You are not going outside to that cemetery tonight. If you even try it, I'll tell Aunt Kate everything!" There was raw panic in her voice.

"Relax, I'm not stupid," Brad said sarcastically. "The graveyard can wait until the light of day. I have no more desire to meet that Halloween reject in the dark than you do!" He gave a shaky laugh. "Less probably!"

Dru slumped in relief, then yawned. She jumped off the bed, and headed for the door.

"Hey!" Brad said in alarm. "Where're you going?"

"To get my pillow," said Dru. "I'm sleeping in here with you tonight."

"Good!" said Brad. There was genuine relief in his voice. "You can put your blanket on the rug here beside the bed."

"Are you crazy? I'm not about to sleep on the floor!"

"Where are you sleeping, then?"

"Right there with you."

Brad hesitated. "Okay," he agreed grudgingly. He yawned sleepily. "Just don't plan on making a habit of it."

"Don't worry," Dru answered over her shoulder. "There are some things worse than ghosts!"

## ADALICIA

The next afternoon Brad stood in the small front parlor watching Dru's somehow furtive movements in the rapidly darkening afternoon. The sun threw a slanted, western light through the pocked old glass of the parlor windows. The last few beams cast a lurid, underwater glow on Dru's face. She was kneeling in front of Aunt Kate's small walnut desk, and was so engrossed in what she was doing that she didn't hear Brad enter the room. She was pressing a knot hole on the back of one of the drawers so hard that her knuckles were white and her thumb seemed almost disjointed.

"What are you doing, Dru?" Brad asked sharply.

"Oh!" She was so startled that she jumped and the drawer clattered to the floor.

"Don't sneak up on me like that!" she exclaimed angrily.

"I didn't sneak up on you! I merely entered the parlor of my own home and found my sister poking a knot hole. What are you doing, anyhow?"

"I'm poking this knothole, stupid!" Dru snapped. Her breath was still coming in sharp jerks. She picked up the drawer again.

"I can see that," said Brad. "May I ask why?"

"Listen, Brad!" said Dru abandoning the argument. "I've figured it out. The secret has to be in this desk. According to Aunt Kate, this is the most important antique in the house. It belonged to the original Colonel Brannock. It's made of black walnut taken from the property. It was cut at a local mill, and designed and made by a local craftsman. It's been here since day one. It's a real big deal!"

"So? You think the ghost cares about that?"

"No, but I think if there's a map or a letter or something, it has to be in a secret drawer in this desk. It's the only logical place. That's why I'm pressing this knothole. They sometimes disguise hidden locks. I've already looked inside all the drawers. There's nothing in them but Aunt Kate's papers: bills, receipts, things like that. There's got to be a false bottom in back of one of them. Help me look! I've already examined the desk. There's a secret compartment inside, behind the top drawer, but it's pretty simple and there's nothing in it. It may have been designed to throw people off the track."

"Okay," said Brad, interested in spite of himself. "But we'd better hurry. Aunt Kate's bound to come home soon and I don't want to have to explain all this to her," he said, waving his hands toward the stacks of papers on the floor. "Where is she, anyway?"

"She went over to Sarah's house to help Mrs. Pollock with a report for the Historical Society. Sarah is going to type it for them when they're finished."

"Oh?" said Brad with interest. "I'd better develop my pictures of Brannock Hall. Aunt Kate may need them."

"What's this sudden interest in local history?" Dru asked suspiciously. "I thought you didn't care about anything invented before 1985."

"I just think I need to do my part toward supporting Aunt Kate. After all, we are living in her house."

"Very kind of you!" said Dru wickedly. "And how much support will Sarah need during those long, exhausting hours she spends typing?"

Brad was spared an answer by the sound of Aunt Kate's car wheels on the loose gravel driveway.

"Here she comes!" whispered Dru urgently. "Let's hope she parks the car in the stable. That'll give me time to clean up this mess."

She was already hurriedly placing the papers back in the drawers. "Quick!" she whispered. "You go outside and delay Aunt Kate somehow. I won't need much time. I know where everything goes. I can push the desk back against the wall by myself."

When Brad entered the front door a few minutes later, chatting with Aunt Kate and carrying a stack of books, Dru was standing in the middle of the room with a wide smile on her face. Brad cast a quick glance around the parlor. It was as neat as ever, but Dru seemed slightly out of breath.

"There you are!" she said heartily. "Both of you. I was really getting worried! It's really great when we're all together! Here, let me help you with those books. Did you enjoy your afternoon with Mrs. Pollock? Did you get a lot done? What're we having for supper? I can hardly wait. I'm starving!"

For just a fraction of a second, Aunt Kate gave Dru a suspicious look but she answered calmly, "I'm sorry I was a little late getting home. We can begin supper right away, if you'd like. You and Brad set the table while I open a jar of spaghetti sauce and fix a salad."

Dru followed her to the kitchen, giving Brad a relieved glance. As the three of them worked preparing the meal, she listened quietly to Brad and Aunt Kate's conversation. She was a little puzzled by Brad's good humor after what had happened the night before. He was so frightened that she had expected him to be somehow different today. Instead, he seemed completely normal - even cheerful. She sighed. Brad always fooled you. She would be lucky if he would even discuss the ghost with her tonight. Brad was like that. He sometimes operated on the principle that unpleasant things would go away if you ignored them long enough. She remembered a library book he "forgot" for four months when he was twelve. It got so he wouldn't even go to the library and claimed he hated the librarian, but she called Mom and complained. When he finally returned the book, he had to pay a five dollar fine. The only reason he didn't owe more was because there was a limit on each book.

Dru watched him as he grinned at Aunt Kate and filched one of the meatballs she was spooning onto a plate. She could see the old library book philosophy developing, but she was determined to get to the bottom of the mystery. She wished she could talk to Aunt Kate. It would actually be a relief to turn the whole thing over to an adult, but she felt that what Brad said the night before was probably true. If Aunt Kate's safety depended on her knowing nothing about the ghost, they had no right to place her in jeopardy.

While they ate, Dru eyed her closely. At last she spoke, choosing her words carefully. "Aunt Kate, how do you know so much about the history of Brannock Hall?"

Aunt Kate looked at her with interest. "When Mama and I moved to Brannock Hall thirty years ago, we found three old trunks full of letters and papers in the attic. I had always been interested in the history of Brannock Hall, but nobody had any idea there were trunks full of newspapers and letters hidden away all those years. Fortunately, the roof never leaked, and the trunks stayed dry.

Mama and I spent years going through the contents of two of the trunks. We found a treasure trove of family and county history, and we studied and cataloged it all. We donated the most valuable papers to the state historical museum in Raleigh."

"What did they say?" asked Brad with interest.

"Well, the first two trunks dealt mainly with Colonel Brannock's days. He died in 1840 and left Brannock Hall to his oldest son, Robert. Robert's wife died when she was very young, leaving one daughter, Adalicia, who was just a baby when her mother died. She was supposed to have been very beautiful."

"Oh!" breathed Dru. "What happened to her?"

Aunt Kate hesitated, looking at Brad and Dru's eager faces. "I don't really know," she answered. "Robert was killed in a small fight near Kinston in 1862 during the early years of the war, but by that time Adalicia was already dead. She was only sixteen when she died. When I was a child, I remember hearing of some mystery surrounding her death, but I don't remember what it was. Mama would never talk about it to me, and I never felt I should force her. I've wondered all these years if the third trunk, the one we never explored, might hold the secret of Adalicia's death."

Dru and Brad were fascinated. They wanted to hear more. "But, what happened to Brannock Hall after Robert died?" asked Brad.

"After Robert's death, the property passed on to his younger brother, Webb, but he never lived in it. He inherited it during the Civil War and the overseer, a man named Jacque LeFevre, managed it while Robert and Webb were fighting. After the war, times were hard in Brannock County because the economy had been destroyed. Most of the other great houses had been burned by the Yankees, but for some reason Brannock Hall escaped destruction. Webb survived the war and had a large family. You'd have thought he'd have welcomed the chance to live at Brannock Hall and farm the land, but for some reason he chose to live in town. Brannock Hall was never farmed again. People said there was some kind of blight on the property, and there were rumors of ghosts and strange lights. No Brannock lived here again until Mama and I moved in."

She snorted. "What nonsense!" In 30 years, Mama and I never so much as experienced even one unexplained happening. There were occasional night noises, especially at first, but every old house settles with the changes in temperature, and we got used to it. I don't even notice it now. Most of the property was sold before Mama inherited the house, but we've rented the corn field beside the stable for years and it's been very fertile." She looked with amusement at Brad and Dru. "We all know there's no ghost at Brannock Hall."

Dru and Brad kept their faces blank and carefully avoided each other's eyes.

"Aunt Kate," ventured Dru after a short silence. "Weren't you terribly curious about Adalicia and all the rumors. Why didn't you and Great-Grandmother open the third trunk?"

"Why," said Aunt Kate matter-of-factly. "It took us nearly thirty years to finish going through the first two. Remember, I was teaching all those years and I simply didn't have a lot of extra time; and after that, Mama got sick. I just haven't gotten around to the third one yet."

There was a few moments of silence as Brad and Dru absorbed this news. "Aunt Kate," ventured Dru again. "Where are the trunks now? Is it possible that Brad and I could see some of the papers?"

"Of course. I'll take you up to the attic to-morrow and you can spend as much time as you like. It's wonderful to have you and Brad interested in the family history! So many young people today are interested only in computers and loud music. They seem to have lost the appreciation for their heritage." Dru gave Brad a hard look. He was examining his fingernails.

Tonight Dru was glad when dinner was over and homework was done, and she and Brad could relax in their rooms. They had a lot to discuss.

"Dru," said Brad lazily, "turn yours up a little."

Dru reached over to the radio playing quietly beside her bed and adjusted the volume until it blended exactly with the sounds of Brad's coming through the hole. They did this often at night, listening to music and talking quietly until they drifted off to sleep.

"I wish we'd known about the attic papers earlier," Dru said. "It's strange Aunt Kate hasn't mentioned them before now."

"That's because she doesn't want us to go in the attic. She has an insane uncle she keeps locked in a closet up there. He's hiding from the Yankees, and he wears women's clothes and a long, gray wig. She doesn't give him anything to eat but bread and water, and he doesn't get any sun so his skin is white and withered. He stinks!"

"Sure," said Dru with a yawn. "If he escaped from the Yankees, he'd be about one hundred and fifty years old."

"He is," answered Brad solemnly.

"Right!" said Dru in disgust. "What genius told you that?"

"Aaron Clark," Brad answered with mock seriousness.

"Well, that explains it! I'd rather find a smelly, insane hundred and fifty year old Confederate soldier up there than Aaron!"

Brad grinned to himself, but he answered seriously, "You'll see tomorrow."

The next morning after breakfast, Aunt Kate opened a door at the opposite end of the hall from their bedrooms and led them up a narrow flight of steps neatly covered with black rubber matting. The attic was large and spotlessly clean, and sunlight streamed in from the windows under the eaves. Metal utility shelves lined one wall at the western end of the attic, and two long tables stood on a square of carpet. On the shelves were piles of albums and flat document boxes which were neatly numbered and cataloged. The entire area looked like an efficient office with containers of sharpened pencils and boxes of paper clips. Placed against the wall, and looking out of place, were three enormous, black, battered trunks.

"There," said Aunt Kate, looking around. "I haven't had the heart to come up here in months, but Mama and I spent many hours up here together. Most of the early history of this state was in those trunks. It was a job getting through them, but the papers were invaluable. I'm going to trust you with them," she said, giving Brad and Dru a piercing look.

It was Brad who spoke. "You can trust us to take care of them, Aunt Kate. I mean that."

She nodded, satisfied. "Now," she continued. "I'll be out most of the morning, but I'll be home for lunch." She turned and walked briskly down the stairs. "Don't bring any food up here," she called as she closed the door at the bottom of the steps. "I don't want to attract rats and roaches."

Brad and Dru stood looking at each other. "Thirty years!" said Brad in despair. "By the time we look through this stuff even the ghost will be dead!"

"Oh, I don't know," said Dru. "I have a feeling that what we're looking for is in the third trunk. Aunt Kate's been through the other two and the only family mystery she's mentioned is Adalicia who died just before the Civil War. She says all the Civil War stuff is in the third trunk."

Brad did not look much happier. "Well, even if it takes us only fifteen years, Dru, we'll still be too old to care!" He plopped down on a chair and put his head in his hands.

Dru walked over to the third trunk and lifted the lid. The old hinges creaked a little with the effort. She spent a few minutes leafing through some of the papers on top.

"Listen, Brad. Let's put some order into this. We don't have to read every single document and paper like Aunt Kate and Great-Grandmother did. Let's concentrate on those papers which involve the period of time when Adalicia was alive."

"Why?" asked Brad disconsolately. "How can we be sure Adalicia, or whatever her name was, concerns the ghost at all?"

"We can't, but we have to start somewhere. Do you have a better idea?"

"No," answered Brad unhappily, "but it seems like a lot of work. Do we even know exactly when she lived?"

"Well, we know her father inherited Brannock Hall in 1840 before she was born, and we know she died before the Civil War which started in 1861. That's only about a twenty year period."

"Okay," said Brad, glad of a plan of action. "We'll make piles: 'yes,' 'no,' and 'maybe.' Give me a stack!"

At first they found the job harder than they had expected. The old papers were yellow and brittle and had to be handled with extreme car. The handwriting was tiny and cramped, and the ink had faded to a pale brown over the years. To make things worse, the writer sometimes covered the paper with tiny writing on both sides, and then turned it and wrote vertically across the original text to save paper.

"Don't try to actually read any of them yet, Brad. Just read the date and put it in the proper pile."

"Okay," agreed Brad. "Once you realize the 's' looks like an 'f,' and the '1' looks like a '7,' it's not so hard. But I can't figure out what these little brown blotches all over the papers are."

"I think they must be drops of ink from

their quill pens," Dru guessed.

By lunch time they had separated three large piles of papers. The "no's" they placed carefully back into the bottom of the trunk. They spread a layer of tissue paper on top of them and placed the "maybe's" on top of that. That left the large pile of "yes's" on the floor beside the tables. There were also several stacks of letters tied with string. They didn't bother opening those, but put them with the "yes's."

Brad stretched and did a few jumping jacks. "Let's break and have some lunch," he suggested. "No wonder those people didn't invent TV. They had to spend all their time deciphering their mail. I bet they hated to see the postman!"

Dru laughed. "You go on, Brad. I'll be down in a minute."

She listened as Brad clattered down the steps; then from under a pile of papers she took a small velvet box which she had hidden earlier. She had found it in the trunk. From it she carefully removed a dainty, hinged locket, worked in filigreed gold and hung on a heavy gold chain. In it was a tiny, oval portrait of a girl whose features were almost too small to make out in the attic light. She wanted to see it in the daylight, and for some reason which she could not explain, she wanted to see it alone before she showed it to Brad. The glimpse she had gotten of the tiny face had moved her strangely.

In the kitchen she found Brad and Aunt Kate chattering companionably as they opened a package of hot dogs. She walked through the kitchen to the back porch where she stood blinking in the blinding midday sun, waiting for her eyes to adjust. She carefully removed the locket from its case and gazed at the little painted figure.

In the sunlight, the colors glowed like tiny jewels. The face of a girl about sixteen years old gazed back at her. She was dressed in a pale blue antebellum gown with a deeply scooped neck. Her dark hair was swept away from her face and pulled back into a loose bun. Curling tendrils fell softly around her ears and the nape of her neck. A strand of pearls was intertwined in her hair and gleamed palely against the dark mass of curls. Though her body was angled slightly to the left, her small head was tilted so that she looked directly at the painter. Her left hand rested on her lap with her long, tapered fingers caressing her silk skirt. Her right arm gracefully crossed her body and her hand held, near the curve of her neck, a perfect rosebud.

Dru caught her breath. She was enchanted! The eyes, fringed in dark lashes, were so direct and blue. Her head was held with such grace and courage. The artist had caught the girl's beauty and her intelligence, which gleamed from this tiny surface. Yet as she gazed at the face, Dru was seized by an uneasy feeling. There was something familiar about the face! Something she couldn't quite place.

"Wow!" whistled Brad. "Where did you find that?" He took the locket from her hands and stood gazing at it. "What a beauty!" he almost whispered.

"Yes," agreed Dru. "She was in the trunk, but there's no name on the locket. Let's show her to Aunt Kate."

In the kitchen, Aunt Kate took the locket and examined it thoughtfully. "I had no idea this existed," she said. "It's Adalicia, of course. It must have been copied from the large portrait her father commissioned. It's in the attic. Come with me, and I'll show it to you."

Once more in the airy attic, she led them to a corner under the eaves where she removed a blanket from a large, ornate frame. Brad and

Dru lifted the portrait and carried it to the window where they could examine it in the light. At first glance, they were disappointed. The portrait had hung for many years in the home of one of the Brannock relations. It had been covered with layers of protective shellac which had darkened over the years and given it that dim, mysterious look like pictures in museums; yet, nothing could hide the radiant personality of the girl who gazed with such courage from the canvas. From the murky background, the color of the rose, though muted, still glowed like a tiny banner.

Aunt Kate, who had been quietly looking at the portrait, suddenly exclaimed. "Those must be the Brannock pearls she's wearing in her hair! They were given to Colonel Justin Brannock by the Tuscarora Indians who lived in this part of the state in appreciation for his protection. Each pearl was perfectly matched, and they were priceless - even in those days. Nobody knows what happened to them. They disappeared long ago."

Dru was listening to her in fascination. Her eyes were glowing with interest, and she was straining to hear every word. "How about the rose, Aunt Kate? Is there a reason she is holding the rosebud so high?"

Aunt Kate thought for a moment before she answered. "I think so, but I can hardly remember. I believe there used to be a rumor that Adalicia's mother called her baby daughter 'Little Rosebud,' and when Adalicia was older and very beautiful, people called her the 'Rose of Brannock County.'"

Brad, who had been unusually thoughtful, suddenly exclaimed, "I've got it! It's Sarah! Sarah Pollock looks exactly like Adalicia Brannock!"

"Yes!" exclaimed Dru. "That's it! That's what's been bothering me. It is Sarah Pollock! If Sarah swept her hair back from her face, she could pass for her easily!"

"Well, I declare!" exclaimed Aunt Kate. "I do believe you're right. It never occurred to me before. Of course, I haven't seen this old portrait in years. I've kept it up here where it's dry until I found the time to do something with it."

"But, Aunt Kate!" exclaimed Dru. "Is Sarah a Brannock?"

"Oh, yes! All the old families intermarried. The Brannocks and the Pollocks have been marrying each other for generations. In fact, I believe Sarah's great-great-grandmother married the younger son of Randolph Brannock, one of Justin's younger sons."

"Well, that explains it," said Brad. "Adalicia's genes have popped out all over Sarah. It's a good thing she didn't have a hooked nose and large warts!"

Dru laughed. "I can't wait to show Sarah. May we bring her up here, Aunt Kate?"

"Of course. Sarah's welcome to come whenever she wants."

"Yeah!" agreed Brad enthusiastically. "I bet she'd really have fun looking through these old papers and things. After all, the Brannocks are practically her family, too."

"Right!" said Dru sarcastically. "You'd have a lot more fun up here, too, wouldn't you?"

"Of course!" Brad answered with a grin.

# DARK ROOM

Brad whistled as he walked down the deserted school corridor. He stopped between the two rows of lockers and swung his tennis racket in an imaginary serve. His form was perfect, his grip was strong, his eyes fixed firmly on the ball. His follow-through was a work of art. "All right!" he exclaimed as the ball landed low and hard in the back left corner of the opposing court. It was unreturnable! He gave a little victory dance as he tossed the racket in his locker and snapped it shut. This was what he had been waiting for all day. School was out, tennis practice was over, and the dark room was his for the rest of the afternoon.

He had arrived at school early that morning and prepared his roll of film. It had taken only a few minutes to soak the roll in the C41 developer and rinse it. He had left it hanging to dry during the school day, and now he could finish the job.

It was about time, too. He had been forced to wait for an opportunity to reserve the dark room in his own name, and now, almost a month after he had taken the shots of Brannock Hall, he was ready to develop the film.

He took the steps to the second floor two at a time. He stopped in front of the closet door and fished the key from the pocket of his tennis shorts. He inserted the key in the door, then paused and took a deep breath before opening it. He loved this! But he must be careful not to let his excitement interfere with his memory. Each step was important and everything had to be timed exactly.

The closet was a small one. Shelves had been added on either side to hold the plastic jugs of chemicals and the developing trays. In front of him, on a TV cart, stood the enlarger. Its opaque base gleamed dully.

With a pair of tongs, he lifted the film from the drying rack and carefully snipped it into sections. He randomly selected one of the pieces and inserted it into the tiny frame on the enlarger. He snapped on the small bulb and adjusted the focus knob. There, projected on the opaque base was the negative image of his film. He concentrated on achieving an exact focus. He fixed his eyes on a figure in the foreground and made minute adjustments with the knob. When he was satisfied, he stepped back and gazed for the first time at the entire picture.

It took a moment to adjust to the reversed lighting of the negative image. He grinned as he tried to make out the three figures sitting around the kitchen table. The one with the mass of white hair hanging down her back must be Sarah. Dru's smooth, ash blond hair appeared a dark helmet. His own shock of dark hair fell over his forehead in a white wave. Their white eyes stared weirdly from dark sockets, and the pale shadows on their faces and arms gave them all a disembodied, floating appearance.

Suddenly, he frowned. What was that dark smudge behind Sarah? He turned the knob and focused slightly, but he couldn't make it out.

"Jeez!" In his irritation he spoke aloud. He must have put his finger over the lens.

Still frowning, he checked his focus, centered the image on the base, and turned off the lights. By the red glow of the safe light, he removed a sheet of photographic paper from a heavy envelope and placed it in the easel. He then flicked on the enlarger's bulb to expose the paper, and slowly counted to four. Working quickly, he removed the paper and placed it into the tray of chemical developer.

Standing in frozen horror, he watched as the picture began to emerge through the clear liquid. There around Aunt Kate's kitchen table were the three of them: Dru, Sarah, and himself. He remembered the exact moment. The camera had caught him just as he over-balanced and was toppling backward. His arms were thrown up and his legs were thrown outward. On his face was an expression of surprised alarm, and Sarah and Dru were laughing hysterically.

It was a bright moment, frozen by the camera, but there behind Sarah's head was the faint glow of a white, formless figure. It was wearing a long robe and a hood which covered its face. Brad felt the now familiar prickling on the back of his neck. He glanced apprehensively around the small dark closet. The red glow from the safe light suddenly seemed sinister, and he fought the urge to burst out the door and run screaming down the hall.

He took several deep breaths. "Be calm!" he told himself. "It's only a picture." But he couldn't help holding it at arms length between his thumb and forefinger as he transferred it from the developer to the stop-bath tray. Despite his pounding heart, he forced himself to time each procedure carefully. He disciplined himself to transfer the print to the fixer for two minutes and finally to the water bath where it would sit for ten minutes. As he stared at it through the slight distortion of the clear water, he forced himself to think logically.

The figure was almost ridiculously like everybody's idea of a ghost. It was pale and faint like white smoke, and he could vaguely make out the lines of the kitchen counter visible behind it. Even though it had no distinct form, its basic shape was human. Its face was hidden beneath the hood, but its head was tilted down toward Sarah seated in front of it.

Why Sarah? Why had it appeared while Aunt Kate was in the room? He and Dru had convinced themselves that they were all safe when Aunt Kate was around. Then why had it appeared in the kitchen that day?

The answer, of course, was that it had not actually appeared. None of them had seen or sensed it, and if he and Dru were right, it would not appear in any of the prints which pictured Aunt Kate. The thought spurred him into action. He had better develop the rest of the roll and see if he were right.

Quickly he snapped on the over-head light and inserted the next negative in the enlarger's frame. For the next hour, he worked quickly and efficiently, focusing each negative and exposing it, then processing the paper through the developer and water bath.

As he worked, he could see a definite pattern emerging. The figure appeared in every print which contained Sarah, as long as Aunt Kate was not in the picture, too. It never appeared in a picture which did not contain Sarah, and it never appeared in a picture which did contain Aunt Kate. Sometimes in the shadow beneath the hood, he could see the gleam of its eyes. It gave Brad the shivers to think that on that January afternoon, his first truly happy day at Brannock Hall, they had been stalked by this horror. Despite his forced calmness, he could not shake a growing feeling of menace.

The last half of the roll contained the shots he had taken of Brannock Hall for Aunt Kate. The first few were of different angles of the house, and Brad spared a moment of pride when he noticed how sharp the lines of the old home appeared in the clear light of the winter afternoon. The last shot was the one he had taken of the cemetery just as the sun was setting.

"I knew it!" thought Brad.

As he focused the negative in the enlarger, he could already make out the ghost in one corner. He stood very quietly and looked at the developed print through the water bath. A few minutes later, there it stood; glowing eyes under the hood fixed intently on the camera. It was standing slightly to the right of one of the old yews on the left hand edge of the cemetery. It was the exact spot and exact pose of the figure he had seen that first night at Brannock Hall.

Brad was too exhausted to react. With the last of his strength, he removed the print from the water bath and clamped it with the others to dry on the overhead rack. As he stumbled out of the room and carefully locked the door behind him, he had only two thoughts: he had a lot to tell Dru, and he had to be at school at dawn the next day to retrieve the dried prints before anyone else saw them!

## THE ROSE STONE

Brad ate dinner silently, paying little attention to Dru and Aunt Kate's conversation. Several times he was aware that they were looking at him inquiringly, and was grateful they left him alone. He had to hand it to Aunt Kate. She never smothered you with attention.

He was too restless to settle down to homework after dinner, and was glad when Dru suggested they go up to their rooms and listen to the radio, though he hated to leave the safety of Aunt Kate's presence. Now that he knew the ghost was always with them, he felt as if there were a hidden camera watching his every move. Maybe Aunt Kate emitted invisible rays that created a force field, and disabled the ghost's power. He shook himself. This was serious!

As soon as they climbed the stairs, he

beckoned Dru into his room. He looked both ways down the hall and closed the door behind them. It was irrational, he knew. Closed doors obviously didn't stop this ghost, but it was hard to shake the physical laws of the everyday world.

"What's going on, Brad?" Dru asked. "You were so quiet during supper, and you hardly ate a thing."

She listened intently as he told her what had happened that afternoon. When she spoke her voice was low with horror and she could feel the creepy sensation of goose bumps breaking out all over her skin. "You must have been terrified, Brad!"

He answered honestly. "The first one really frightened me! When I saw the dark smudge behind Sarah in the negative, I thought it was my thumb; but when I saw the figure of the ghost emerging, I almost bolted! It took me a while to calm down, I can tell you that!"

Dru was impressed by his seriousness. She could tell just how frightened he had been. "Did it look like the same thing that shook your bed that night?"

"Yes, I'm sure it was." He thought for a moment. "But, Dru, seeing a white smudge on a photograph, and seeing the actual ghost in person are two different things. It wasn't the appearance of the ghost that frightened me that night, it was the ghost's presence, it's power!" Brad shuddered involuntarily. He still found talking about that night difficult.

Dru sounded worried. "I don't like the ghost hanging around Sarah. Do you think it wants to hurt her?"

Brad was silent for a long time. "You know, I don't think it does. Somehow it didn't appear to be menacing her. In one of the shots it seemed to be pointing to her and beckoning to me, but I think if it wanted to hurt her, it would've done it already. It's strong enough!"

He glanced at the heavy wooden bed, and remembered how easily the ghost had tossed it around.

"I can't wait for you to see the shot taken in the cemetery. It's exactly what I've been trying to describe for weeks. It's the only shot where the ghost's eyes are clearly visible, and it'll give you the creeps!"

"Did you say it's the only shot where its eyes are showing, Brad?" she asked with a note of excitement in her voice.

"Yes," said Brad, puzzled.

"Don't you see? That's a clue! It must be

an important spot."

"But Dru, we've been in the cemetery. We searched all through it the day after the ghost appeared in my bedroom. There's nothing in there but graves of Indians and slaves. We even matched the broken gravestones to their bases and found nothing unusual. If there's a clue there, we're too stupid to figure it out!"

"You may be," said Dru, "but I'm not! Why don't we go back in there tomorrow and concentrate on the spot where the ghost has appeared twice now. If his eyes are as big as you say they are, he's probably trying to tell you something."

"You make him sound like a puppy dog," said Brad in disgust, "with pleading, dark eyes. Dru, this thing doesn't plead! It glares!"

"Well, Mrs. Shapiro used to glare at you and Aaron all the time, and that never slowed you down. It won't hurt to look in the cemetery one more time. Do you have a better idea?"

"No," admitted Brad grumpily, "but I'll bet we don't find anything."

He felt better, though. Somehow talking things over with Dru had been a relief. She was a little like a small, blond Aunt Kate, he thought; she somehow brought things back down to reality.

The next morning Brad woke with a jerk. He noted with approval the early gray dawn just visible through his window. His clock showed exactly 5:00. He sprang out of bed in a single leap and reached for the shirt and jeans he had slung on his chair the night before.

"Dru!" he hissed loudly. "Get up! We've got to get moving!"

He could hear her bed squeak as she turned over. She groaned softly.

"I'm not waiting for you!" he hissed. "I've got to explore the cemetery and get to the school early before someone else opens the dark room and finds the pictures."

He worked hurriedly, pulling on socks and shoes. He could hear Dru stumbling sleepily around in her room, but when he opened his door and walked softly toward the steps, she was close behind him, hair tousled and face still puffy from sleep. She didn't have his talent for early rising, he thought with satisfaction, but she was determined to explore the cemetery with him. She would come back later and finish dressing while he biked to school.

The gray dawn was chilly and the grass wet under their feet as they walked across the lawn to the cemetery. They stood for a moment at the black iron gate and looked inside. It was strange, Brad reflected, how the mood of the cemetery changed in different lights. Here in the early March dawn, the heavy yew branches with their thick swathes of Spanish moss trapped a slight ground mist. The thin, narrow stones seemed to float eerily between the gray mist from the ground and the gray moss hanging from the trees. It was spooky, he thought. No wonder people make up so many stories about ghosts and old graveyards. He shivered slightly; he didn't like this place. It frightened him.

He glanced at Dru who looked a little perkier. She was gazing with interest at the corner where the ghost had stood. Brad wondered momentarily if it were safe to let her get so involved. Dru seemed entirely unafraid of the ghost, but she had never seen it. For a second his mind flashed back to the night the ghost appeared in his bedroom. There was power there - and danger! The ghost was more than a white smudge in a photograph. It was real.

Dru broke the silence. "I have an idea. I think we need to start over there by that tree," she said, pointing to a tree on the left. "That's where you've seen it twice: once the night we arrived, and once in the picture. You wait here and I'll go inside. You can tell me when you think I'm standing in the right place."

As usual, Brad had to admit, Dru came up with a good, sensible plan, and he was interested in spite of himself. He watched as she walked slowly toward the twisted old yew, her feet disappearing in the swirling mist.

"There!" he called. "Stop right there! Now, move about two feet backward." He stood gauging her angle like an artist, trying to superimpose on Dru's position the exact spot where the ghost had stood. "I think that's it!" he called.

He pushed open the gate and stepped inside. The mist wasn't as thick as it appeared from outside, and he could clearly see the fallen gravestones through it. He walked over to Dru and both turned in small circles staring stupidly at the ground. Brad was suddenly flooded with depression. He felt the bones in his legs melt as he collapsed to the ground. Nothing! Absolutely nothing!

"This was it," he thought. "This was somehow their last chance."

Dru had pushed aside the low branches of the yew, and was forcing her way inward.

"Come on!" she panted. "Help me bend these branches! There's got to be something here."

Springing up, Brad pushed his way toward Dru and using his wiry strength, seized a large, low branch and pushed it slowly to one side.

"Keep going!" Dru screamed in excitement. "I see something!"

Brad turned around and set his back to the branch. Then, gritting his teeth, he pushed backward with all his strength. As the branch slowly swept to one side, they could see a small marble stone, about twelve inches square, embedded in the ground. It was dirty and covered with lichen, but the clear, white marble with it's pink veining still showed through in spots. There was no writing on it, no words or dates, but clearly embossed on the cold, pink stone was a beautiful marble rosebud.

Dru and Brad stared at it in shocked surprise. Then meeting each other's eyes, they exclaimed in unison, "Adalicia!"

Brad was suddenly aware of the strain in his trembling legs. "Move!" he shouted to Dru. "I've got to let go! I can't hold it any longer!"

Dru skipped out to the open, and Brad lifted his feet and let the branches snap together. He shoved his way through the thick, yew needles until he stood facing Dru. They didn't need to speak. The beautiful piece of marble with it's dainty rosebud had to mark Adalicia's grave. But why was she, the daughter of a Southern plantation owner, lying here among her father's slaves?

A few minutes later, Dru watched as Brad peddled furiously down the drive. He leaned away from the curve as he took the corner, and she momentarily glimpsed his body bent over the handlebars before the crepe myrtles hid him from view. It would be a disaster if someone else discovered the pictures, but if all went well, he would be waiting at the front entrance before Mr. Anderson arrived, and could race up to the second floor.

As she walked toward the house, her mind whirled. She was worried about Sarah. Somehow, Sarah and Adalicia were all mixed up together, and there was something very sinister going on. It was obvious from the pictures that the ghost was stalking Sarah, and she didn't like to think that Sarah was in danger when she visited them. She had seen other pictures of Sarah, and the only ones with ghosts in them were the ones taken at Brannock Hall. It made sense that the ghost only stalked her here. They'd have to find some excuse to keep Sarah away until they figured out what was going on. Actually, that shouldn't be too hard. Sarah was the most popular girl in school, and besides being president of the freshman class, was also a cheerleader. She didn't have a lot of extra time.

As Dru climbed the back steps, she could hear Aunt Kate clattering around in the kitchen. Aunt Kate always fixed a big breakfast with grits and biscuits and sliced tomatoes. At first Dru had rebelled, but now she looked forward to it.

She entered her room still lost in thought. Brad would have to spend more time with Sarah at her house. He wouldn't mind that! This might actually give him the chance he needed. Dru was puzzled by Brad's attitude toward Sarah. She had never known him to be shy around a girl before. He spent a lot of time looking at Sarah, but he never got up the courage to ask her out. He was acting so funny!

Last Monday, Dru was getting a book from her locker. She was hidden by the open locker door, and had seen Brad without his knowing it. It was between classes, and Sarah was standing with a group of her friends. Just then, Brad walked by, and Sarah turned and gave him a smile that lit up the hall. Everyone noticed but Brad. He merely waved and walked on by. Dru was amazed by Sarah's reaction. She stood quietly for a moment, then walked abruptly away. Well, now Brad was going to have to make a move! Sarah needed him.

She stared sightlessly out the window. They needed a plan. Up to now they had been gathering information by bits and pieces, but a pattern was beginning to emerge.

"What do we really know about the ghost?" she thought.

Brad was frankly afraid and had an emotional reaction whenever he thought about it, but she had never seen it, and could be more objective.

First, despite its frightening manifestations, it had never tried to hurt any of them, though Brad was convinced of its pent-up strength. She reviewed its various appearances. It did not seem to hold a particular hatred toward any of them. It had frightened Brad several times, but rather than menacing him, it seemed to be trying to get his attention - perhaps even his help. Why Brad?

"Because it feels Brad is more able to help it," she thought. She gave a short laugh. "A male chauvinist ghost!"

Second, they suspected there was a connection between the ghost and Adalicia. It had shown them the spot in the slave cemetery where the tree branches had grown over Adalicia's grave. There is something we are supposed to learn about Adalicia.

"Okay!" she thought. "We're doing that already."

She remembered the long hours she and Brad (especially she) had spent among the papers in the attic. They had poured over the fine, cramped, brown handwriting in the old letters until they had headaches. It was agonizingly slow and they no longer were surprised that Aunt Kate and her mother had worked for thirty years on the two trunks they had cataloged.

They were beginning to gain a feeling for Adalicia's family: her beautiful young mother, the serious, sometimes sad, father. Last Saturday, they had translated several letters from friends and family members rejoicing with the parents over the birth of baby Adalicia, but it was too slow. They needed to find a way to move on. There was something they needed to discover - and fast!

"And that was the third thing they knew," thought Dru, with a feeling of panic. That "something" probably involved Sarah. Once you accepted the fact that the ghost had a rational message, you had to accept the fact that everything it revealed was significant. Something nagged at her mind.

Suddenly she glanced at the clock. It was getting late! She'd have to shower and dress and eat in a hurry if she hoped to head Sarah off. Even if the ghost didn't intend to hurt her, there was too much undisciplined power there.

"Just give us a little more time!" she begged aloud. "Just a little more time!"

In a few minutes she ran down the back stairs into the kitchen. Her shining hair was still damp. She plopped down at the table and grabbed a biscuit and began cramming it in her mouth. Aunt Kate looked at her in surprise. Dru guiltily placed the biscuit on her plate and gave Aunt Kate an embarrassed grin.

"Where's Brad?" Aunt Kate asked. "He's usually down before you are."

"Oh, he left hours ago! He wanted to ride his bike to school. He says he needs the exercise."

Aunt Kate snorted. "This is the first time I've known him to pass up food in favor of exercise."

"Oh, it probably won't last long."

She forced herself to eat the hot biscuit slowly. The melted butter oozed inside. It was just right!

"Dru," said Aunt Kate. "I wonder if you would do something for me? I need twenty copies of this paper before my meeting tonight. Would you stop by the high school library and ask Louise Hamilton to copy it for me. She can put it on the Historical Society tab. "Also," she handed Dru an old book with a tattered brown leather binding, "I need an enlargement of the photograph on this page "

"Enlargement!" thought Dru. She forgot copiers could do that. She absently kissed Aunt Kate on her cheek and picked up her book bag and Aunt Kate's papers before heading out the back door. She stopped on the brick walk between the rows of boxwood and laughed aloud.

"Enlarge!" she repeated. "We may have found the way. All it takes is money, and Brad will just have to ante up his share. After all, this involves Sarah!"

In her mind she could already see the cramped brown writing blown up to several times its actual size.

# LETTERS

"Well," said Aunt Kate as she set the dish of fried okra on the table. "Saturday afternoon is a good time to begin working in the old kitchen. "I've made arrangements with Watson's garage to haul away what we don't want. We can clean what we want to keep and store it in the stable."

During this speech, Brad and Dru were exchanging glances. Dru spoke first. "Aunt Kate," she said cautiously, "don't you think we ought to finish the school year and concentrate on our tennis and school work before we start such a big project. Can't the junk in the kitchen wait until summer vacation?"

"Junk!" exclaimed Brad incredulously. "Junk! Why that old kitchen is filled with antiques worth thousands of dollars. Each piece needs to be appraised individually, and we'll have special cards printed with a Brannock Hall logo like they do in the classy antique shops. There'll be people from all over the state who'll want a piece of j..., I mean an antique from Brannock Hall."

Aunt Kate snorted happily. "Hold on, Brad. Maybe I'd better put a ceiling on the amount I promised to let you and Dru split. Perhaps I'd better draw a line at five hundred dollars."

"Five hundred dollars!" exclaimed Brad in amazement. "That old rocking chair I can see through the window will bring in five hundred dollars all by itself. We're going to make thousands! One hundred bucks for a genuine Brannock Hall broom. Two hundred for a butter churn - three if it's not cracked. Four hundred for a plow!" Brad was getting more and more excited. He began to run his fingers through his hair.

Dru looked at him in disgust. "Why don't you put some genuine Brannock Hall cobwebs in sandwich bags and sell them? They should be worth about five dollars apiece."

"You think so?" Brad was half serious.

Aunt Kate looked at him approvingly. "There's a lot of history out there in that old kitchen. I'm glad to have somebody help me sort through it."

"Brad doesn't care about the history of the stuff, Aunt Kate. He cares about the money!"

Aunt Kate gave Brad a pat on his head as she passed. "There's plenty of both, I should think."

"Sickening!" Dru thought to herself. She could see it all now. Brad and Aunt Kate would spend all spring in the kitchen exaggerating the value of the junk, and she'd have to find some excuse to avoid the fun and stick with the letters in the attic. She couldn't give up now just as they were beginning to make progress. She was taking several letters a day to the copy machine in the library and enlarging them, making the tiny, cramped handwriting easier to read. Reading the old letters was like watching a mini-series on TV; each day she learned something different. Things hadn't been the same since Adalicia's mother died. Robert had been overwhelmed by grief, and almost immediately left home, leaving Adalicia behind. Dru was worried about her. She was only two.

Brad caught Dru's eye and suddenly he understood. "Aunt Kate," he said, "the kitchen will have to be a strictly weekend affair until school is out. Dru and I have at least two tough tennis matches, and Dru needs to hit the books regularly to keep her grades up."

Dru was too grateful to him to give this last remark the disgust which it deserved. She stood behind Aunt Kate's back and smiled at him.

"Of course," said Aunt Kate as she rose from the table with a dish in each hand. "I never expected anything else."

After they had finished cleaning the dishes, Brad followed Dru upstairs. They sat companionably for a while, each lost in their own thoughts. Brad spoke first, and Dru wasn't surprised to find that they were thinking the same thing.

"Dru," he said," Adalicia must have had a lonely childhood. It was sad how often her father was away from home."

"Yeah," she agreed. "When his wife died, he seemed to have left home for good. He practically raised Adalicia by letter."

In the trunk they had found three thick stacks of papers tied in faded pink ribbon. There were hundreds of letter from Robert Brannock to Adalicia which they called the "Papa" letters. At first they were as difficult to decipher as all the others, but after the first two or three they became easier. They always started with a few words of affection, followed by advice like "be a good girl," and "do your lessons." They usually concluded with wishes that they could be together, and were always signed, "Your Loving Papa." They stretched over a period of about fourteen years, which was most of Adalicia's lifetime after her mother died.

Dru and Brad had been saddened by them. They could picture the beautiful child pouring over each letter and then carefully untying the ribbon and adding it to the top of the stack.

There was another group of letters from Robert Brannock to Jack LeFevre, the plantation manager. They appeared to be letters of instruction and business dealings, and they only briefly glanced through them. There was another stack of letters from Jack LeFevre to Robert Brannock. These they had not read at all.

The fourth group of letters, the ones from Adalicia to her father, were the most numerous and by far the most interesting. The very early ones were written in large, childish letters with lots of ink spots. They told what she had done that day, and always ended with the wish of seeing her dear Papa very soon. This last plea always seemed to cry from the heart of a lonely child, and Dru wondered how her father could have resisted it. Holding the letters from the long dead girl had brought tears to Dru's eyes. Even the ones from the tiny Adalicia, still almost a baby, seemed to sparkle with personality.

"I think we're on the right track," Brad spoke. "The key to the mystery must be in those letters."

"Yes," agreed Dru, "I'm going to concentrate on Adalicia's. Now that I am used to her handwriting, they should be easier to read."

"You could probably skip over the childhood ones," suggested Brad. "Whatever happened probably developed the last year or so of her life."

"No," said Dru. "I want to read them all. I want to know her. Somehow, I feel I owe it to her. I know its strange, but she had so few friends that I want to make it up to her." She looked at Brad, daring him to laugh.

But he only nodded slowly. "I know," he said. "There was something special about her."

They sat quietly together, their thoughts turning backward over more than one hundred years to the child who had played in that very room and perhaps slept on that same bed. What had happened to her?

They were so lost in thought that they did not hear the quiet knocking on the walls. They thought the soft sighing sounds were the wind. Their radios played softly, and they drifted off to sleep.

Aunt Kate's plans for Saturday were postponed by a heavy spring rain. Brad was depressed. He needed money, and the kitchen antiques were a sure thing. Dru, however, was delighted.

"It's a perfect opportunity to spend some time in the attic," she insisted. "Besides, what else are you going to do? It's too wet for tennis practice."

Brad grudgingly agreed, and followed her up the steps. Sitting facing Brad, Dru selected one of the letters that lay scattered in small piles on the rug between them.

"Listen to this, Brad! Adalicia wrote it before she was five. There's a woman named Emily who was probably her governess. She was a good one because she taught her to read and write when she was so little. But, Adalicia sounds so lonely."

*March 10, 1848*

*Dearest Papa,*
(read the large, uneven letters)

   *Emily helped me write this letter.*
*Today we shall read together. I missed*
*my papa so yesterday I cried a little.*
*Emily promises to teach me to em-*
*broider a scarf for you. When you*
*wear it you will remember.*

                    *Your Loving Daughter,*
                               *Adalicia*


*March 15, 1848*

*My Dearest Papa,*
   *Today Emily and I read together*
*for the longest time. We began your*
*scarf after dinner. When I get tired*
*and prick my finger, I think of how*
*you will love it.*

                    *Your Loving Daughter*


*March 25, 1848*

*My Dearest Papa,*
   *Today Emily spared a few min-*
*utes to pick flowers with me in the*
*garden, though she was too busy to*
*stay long. They were yellow daisies.*
*We found one blue butterfly. I wanted*

*to save it for you, but Emily said I*
*must let it go because it is wrong to*
*keep it. When you come home, I'll*
*find you another.*
                    *Your Loving Daughter*

Brad interrupted with an exclamation. "Doesn't her father ever come home? Can't he tell how much she needs him? She's only a little girl, stuck out here all by herself in the country without anybody but Emily."

"I don't think so," said Dru. "I haven't found any mention of a visit so far, and I've read through all the letters when she was five and six. Robert came home once when she was seven, but he didn't stay long."

She leafed through a pile of letters, her face serious.

"Nothing much changes for a couple years, but when she's about eight, things get better. Listen!"

She skipped over several letters and selected one near the bottom of the pile.

                              *June 5, 1852*
*My Dearest Papa,*
    *I am so excited! Emily promises*
*Daniel may come play with me. How*

*I look forward to his visit, for though
I love Emily with all my heart, I must
confess I am sometimes a little lonely
without my dearest Papa.*

*Your Loving Daughter*

Brad looked worried. "She needs a friend,"
he said, "but who is this Daniel? Why hasn't
she mentioned him before?"

"You'll see," said Dru with a smile. "I think
he must be one of Emily's relations. He probably lives on some small farm nearby."

*June 10, 1852*

*My Dearest Papa,*

*Today Daniel came! Emily read
and Daniel listened too. Afterwards,
we went to Willow Run and caught
silver minnows. Daniel promises to
teach me to fish. Though I have been
so busy today, I will practice on the
spinet tonight. Emily is teaching me
a lovely new tune. It will be ready for
you when you come home for Christmas.*

*Your Loving Daughter*

*June 15, 1852*

*Dearest Papa,*

*Today was so lovely! Daniel saddled Rainbow and walked about the stable yard with me. At first, I was ever so frightened, but Rainbow was so gentle, and Daniel so careful that I soon lost my fear. Daniel says he will teach me to ride if you say I might. Might I dearest Papa? I am afraid I have quite lost my heart to Daniel and Rainbow, but I will never love them as I love you!*

*Your Loving Daughter*

*July 30, 1852*

*Dearest Papa,*

*Thank you, my dear, dear Papa, for the stunning blue velvet riding habit! I will look ever so fashionable on Rainbow this winter. Emily says my mama had one just like it. When you come home you will see my progress and be so proud! Daniel says I get on so well. Emily declares I must not neglect my studies, so I will bid farewell for now, my dearest Papa.*

*Your Devoted Daughter*

Dru looked up from the yellowed paper and smiled delightedly at Brad. "Oh, I'm so glad she's found a friend and something she loves to do! She seems so much happier now."

"Yes," answered Brad, "and her writing has improved, too. There are only three ink blotches on that letter, and no spelling errors."

"Emily must have loved Adalicia," remarked Dru. "She was the only one who recognized how lonely she was and tried to do something about it."

"Yeah," answered Brad with a slight frown. "I wonder who Daniel was? If he was her age, he sure was patient with her. He seems to have spent a lot of time teaching her things, and if he was older, I wonder why he bothered? I wouldn't have wasted my time with an eight year-old girl."

"Of course not!" Dru said with disgust. "At least not until she turned about fifteen. But times were different then. You forget Southern chivalry and all that. He was probably a young gentleman - something you wouldn't understand."

Brad leapt to his feet. He shuffled back and forth rapidly and jabbed a couple of blows in the air around Dru's face. He flopped back down. "Well, go on. Let's hear some more about your Little Lord Fauntleroy."

For the next two hours, while the heavy spring rain pelted on the roof, they read to each other from the old letters. They laughed at times over the quaint phrasing. Those from the early years went quickly because the writing was large and only one side of the sheet had been used. Adalicia had written to her father regularly. The letters from the tiny Adalicia were so sad and lonely they were depressing, but her life from the time she was eight and found Daniel until she was about thirteen seemed to have formed a comfortable pattern. There were brief gaps in the letters when Robert paid a visit, but they were always short. Emily was her teacher and friend and Daniel her constant companion. They rode and fished and read together. Her letters sparkled with happiness.

They found themselves caught up in the life of the child who had grown up in this very house, and at times they exclaimed over places she mentioned. In one letter, she described to her father a rainy afternoon spent playing with Daniel in the attic.

Brad looked around the airy attic with interest. "It's almost like being in a time machine. Adalicia's letters have beamed us back to the 1850's. Wouldn't it be funny if we heard a voice calling us to come down to lunch, and instead of Aunt Kate, it turned out to be Emily? Do you think there's a dimension outside of real time where all the dead people who ever lived still exist?"

"No, I don't!" said Dru scornfully. "There are too many of them! George Washington would get all mixed up with Napoleon, and Abraham Lincoln would keep bumping into himself as a boy, and a teenager, and a baby, and an old man. The young Abraham Lincoln might not even like the old one and cause all kinds of trouble for him. And then there'd be all those other people, the ones who we never heard of, milling around and getting in each other's way ..."

"Okay! Okay!" said Brad testily. "It was just a thought."

For a while they sat leafing silently through the letters. Dru picked up several and glanced through them lazily, putting them back down again. She randomly selected one written when Adalicia was about twelve. Immediately, her attention was caught.

*Papa!* (It cried.)

   *The most terrible thing! I could not sleep last night, and as the weather was warm, threw a shawl about my shoulders and walked out into the garden. I saw lights and heard cries coming from the direction of the stable and ran to investigate. Papa! Mr. LeFevre and some other men were standing around an enclosed pit beside the stable. At first I could not see what they were doing, but when I got closer, I could see that they were watching two cocks fighting. One of them had bested the other and was pecking and clawing him, even though his poor broken body could no longer get up! When I cried out and ran to help, Mr. LeFevre spoke to me so roughly, Papa, I cannot tell you! He ordered me away, and I had no choice but to return to the house. But, oh Papa, the poor cock! I write to you, Papa, knowing that your kind heart could never countenance such cruelty. Please, please respond as quickly as ever you can!*

                    *Adalicia*

Dru sat quietly holding the letter lost in thought. She glanced at Brad, but he had not seen Sarah's strange reaction the day she fell in the cock pit. It was almost as though Sarah had been re-experiencing something she had seen before. Could it be that this letter was the answer? Had Sarah really been living Adalicia's past, or had she simply read about the cock fights and let her imagination run away with her?

Before she could discuss it with Brad, he rose to his feet and began to stretch.

"It's almost noon," he said. "Let's take a break; get something to eat, and watch some TV. The tennis courts are still too wet for practice."

"Okay," agreed Dru as she placed the letters carefully in a pile. "We've read all the way through eight years of her life. That's over three hundred letters. They're really hard now. She's using both sides of the paper, and writing between the lines. We need a break."

Brad danced backward to the attic door, jabbing the air with his fists, dodging and feinting to avoid imaginary blows.

"Don't close this door next time, Dru. It's stuffy up here and we need the air."

"I didn't. It must have blown shut."

Brad grasped the knob and pulled. The door did not move. "Hey!" he exclaimed, "it's locked!"

"It can't be! There is no lock."

"You're right!" said Brad after a short examination. He pulled again. "It's stuck!"

"Let me try," said Dru. She grabbed the handle and pulled with all her strength. The door would not budge. A growing chill was permeating the room, and a nauseating smell of decay and musk began to pollute the air.

"Uh, oh!" said Brad under his breath. He looked at Dru. His face was white, and small beads of perspiration were breaking out on his forehead.

"Brad!" whispered Dru, as she backed away from the door. "It's getting cold in here, and there's a terrible smell!" She reached out and took his hand. He could feel it trembling.

"Don't make any sudden moves, Dru. Let's see if we can make it to the window."

Their eyes riveted to the closed door, they backed slowly away until they reached the window under the eaves. While Brad stood facing the door, Dru unlocked the window and cautiously raised the sash. She slowly leaned out and looked down. There was a sheer, two-story drop to the ground below.

"Brad!" she whispered, "we can't jump out! We'll die!" "Sh-h-h-h!" he hissed. "See if you can spot Aunt Kate's car. If she's here, she'll be able to help us."

"Okay, hold my legs!"

She leaned way out and craned her neck around the angle of the eaves. "Brad," she whispered, "I can see the stable. Aunt Kate's car isn't there."

"Maybe she parked in the front of the house. It's our only chance. We'll have to scream."

Quickly, they leaned out the window and screamed at the top of their lungs, "Aunt Kate! Aunt Kate! Help us!"

Behind them in the attic there was a rustling noise. A musty, angry wind sprang up. Letters from their careful stacks were blown about the room, and one of Aunt Kate's precious scrapbooks hurtled toward their heads.

"Okay! Okay!" screeched Brad, suddenly angry. "Stop it! Just settle down!"

Surprisingly, the cold wind lessened, but little angry gusts still blew a few papers around the room. They stood hunched forward, their arms unconsciously outstretched to protect each other. They crouched as if frozen; waiting.

Everything was silent, but the air snapped and crackled expectantly.

After a few moments, Dru whispered. "Do you think it's possible it wants us to keep reading Adalicia's letters?"

"I don't know," Brad hissed. He slowly straightened his body, inch by inch. Moving carefully, he leaned down and picked up a paper which lay on the floor beside his feet. He had no idea what was on it.

Looking fearfully around the room, he began to speak: "Dearest Papa," he improvised. "Today Daniel and I will watch TV and play video games. After lunch, we will teach Rainbow to fish." He paused and waited.

There was a rushing noise and a gust of wind ran down the center of the attic, scattering papers as it blew. It rattled the door momentarily, and then blew under it. Immediately, they felt a sense of release! The room felt warmer and the unbearable smell of decay and mold was already fading away.

Dru's face was red and was choking with the laughter she was trying to stifle with her clamped hand. She was almost hysterical, and her laughter was infectious. In a moment, they were both lying on the floor, holding each other and laughing until they were exhausted.

At last Brad groaned and turned to Dru.

"That thing's getting on my nerves!"

Dru shakily got to her feet. "Come on!" she said. "Maybe it'll let us out after we've read a few more letters. We'll have to clean up this mess first. We can't let Aunt Kate see it like this."

"I wish she'd let us bring some food up here," Brad swallowed. "I'm starving, but most of all I want a soda!"

"Don't talk about it."

They spent the next few minutes picking up papers and placing them back on the shelves. At last they settled down on the rug with a sigh and picked up Adalicia's letters.

Almost immediately they found a change in her life. Beginning after Christmas in the January of 1857 when she was thirteen, her letters were full of excitement over the visit of her Aunt Sarah. Almost every letter was full of joy and anticipation. She was extravagantly thankful to her father for arranging the visit. She and Emily threw themselves into a frenzy of house cleaning, and Daniel was pressed into service as a general fetcher and carrier. Cook Mary was consulted about menus and recipes.

One letter begged permission to enter the

wine cellar and select a table wine for Aunt Sarah's first dinner at Brannock Hall.

> *... For I am quite a young lady, now, dearest Papa, and will soon be four- teen. Emily says I may begin pinning my hair up in May, but Daniel laughs at me for wishing to do so. I assure him that, though I must soon don a corset and begin riding side saddle, I will always be his constant friend. Oh, dearest Papa, I do so hope Aunt Sarah will love me, for next to you and Emily and Daniel, I love her more than anybody else in the whole world! I have never known a mother, and to think your own dear sister will soon be here with me makes me hap- pier than I can express!*

Brad looked up and caught Dru's eye. There was a worried crease between her eye- brows.

"I don't like the sound of this." he said.

"I know," agreed Dru. "Something's bound to go wrong! She's too excited."

There was a break of two weeks, and the next letter from Adalicia was brief and subdued. She mentioned that Aunt Sarah seemed tired from her journey and had not yet taken a meal with them. Brad and Dru could imagine the festive welcome meal Adalicia had spent so much time planning lying uneaten on the table. How disappointed she must have been! But she hid it well. She merely expressed concern that Aunt Sarah was "not quite in spirits." She was confident that she would revive as she regained her strength from the journey. Meanwhile, she and Emily and Daniel were being as quiet as they could possibly be for "dearest Aunt Sarah's sake."

Dru quickly reached for the next letter in the stack which was dated only two days later. It was longer than any of her others and seemed hurriedly written. There were several ink stains and the writing was blurred in spots as though something wet had spilled on it.

*My Dearest Papa,*

*I take my pen in hand to inform my dearest Papa of events here which will surely cause you concern. Please believe me when I say I would not disturb you were it not of the utmost importance. Much as I respect Aunt Sarah, and much as I looked forward*

*to her visit here at Brannock Hall, I
fear her stay is not going well.*

*Dearest Papa, it pains me to tell
you that Aunt Sarah is insisting on
changes in our routine here which I
believe have not been sanctioned by
you. I do not think dear Aunt Sarah
realizes your wishes in certain areas,
and the changes she proposes are
painful to us all!*

*In particular, dear Papa, she will
not allow Emily to dine with us at
table, and has banished her to the
kitchen to work with Cook Mary. The
work is too hard for her, and she is
already ill. And, oh Papa, she has sent
Daniel away! She has given him to
Mr. LeFevre as a field hand. My dearest Papa, I do not believe Mr. LeFevre
values Daniel as he ought, and I am
afraid will be unkind to him.*

*I am writing to you because I
know you will soon put all to rights
again. I know when Aunt Sarah realizes your wishes, we will all be as
we were before. She will soon learn
to love Emily and Daniel as we do,
for Emily and Daniel are my family,*

*and next to you I love them more than*
*anybody else in the world - even Aunt*
*Sarah.*

"No!" exclaimed Dru in astonishment. "Brad! Emily and Daniel were slaves!"

"Slaves!" exclaimed Brad. "I don't like this! I really don't like the sound of any of this!"

"Brad, I believe these blurred spots on the letter are dried tears! I believe little Adalicia was crying when she wrote this letter!"

"She's not so little anymore, Dru. She's almost as old as we are!"

Brad suddenly staggered to his feet. He looked pale and there were tight lines around his mouth. "Let's get out of here, Dru!" he gasped. "I can't stand any more of this. I feel the way I do when I'm watching a horror film and can't bear to see what happens next. But this is real! Something horrible is going to happen!"

Dru nodded silently. There were tears in her eyes as she carefully replaced the letter on the stack. She quietly followed Brad out of the attic.

Both were too depressed to notice the door was standing wide open.

## SARAH

The following week was a busy one. They each had an important tennis match, and it seemed as if every teacher decided to schedule a test. They had no time to spend in the attic, but their thoughts were full of events that happened in that house a century and a half ago.

Brad was worried about the ghost. Since the afternoon in the attic last Saturday, they had been hearing unusual noises and bumps, especially at night, and they had found several small things which had been broken. One night at dinner, the musty, rotten odor he and Dru recognized so well had filled the kitchen. Too nauseated to eat, they watched Aunt Kate curiously to see what she would do. She had to smell it! There was no way she couldn't!

"Oh, my!" she exclaimed in disgust, holding a handkerchief to her nose. "A cat must have dragged a dead possum under the house. I'll have to have it removed tomorrow."

The next day, when the exterminating service did find a dead possum under the house, she seemed satisfied. Only Brad and Dru realized that the pitiful pile of bones and dried fur had been dead far too long to account for the strong, musty odor in the kitchen the night before.

Brad was afraid to mention his growing worry to Dru. She still hadn't experienced the power and the terror of the thing. Her encounter with it had been brief. Last Saturday in the attic was as close as she had come to real fright, and that was a minor incident. Brad was worried that she had begun to develop a friendly, protective feeling toward the ghost, and almost seemed to think of it with affection.

"She thinks it's like a playful dog," he thought with disgust.

Yesterday, when he found a pair of his best jeans savagely ripped apart and flung on his bed, she had laughed. But Brad felt there was nothing friendly about the force that was invading their lives. There was a raw power that he sensed was barely being held in check, and nothing or no one could stand in its way once that power was released. It was obvious the spirit wanted something, and that he and Dru were chosen to find out what! It was also obvious to Brad that the ghost was becoming impatient, and that they were all in danger.

At least he was successful in keeping Sarah away from Brannock Hall. He walked her home from the bus almost every afternoon, and the kids at school were beginning to talk. He grinned. He didn't mind that; just as long as the talk was about Sarah and him and not Sarah and some other guy. Obviously, by spending more time with Sarah, he was leaving Dru at home by herself more often. He still felt she was relatively safe as long as Aunt Kate was around, but Aunt Kate wasn't a pet. He couldn't lock her in the house, or keep her on a leash.

He glanced now at Dru as they climbed the steps to the second floor corridor. She looked tired. Tennis practice had been long and the late March afternoons here in North Carolina were hot. They had only a few minutes to get their books from their lockers before Aunt Kate picked them up. It would be a relief not to have to ride the after school activity bus. Both were glad it was a Friday afternoon. Even the prospect of spending several hours in the attic didn't disturb him, and Aunt Kate was determined to start on the old kitchen this weekend. Brad's spirits lifted a little. He needed the cash.

Suddenly, they were disturbed by the sound of angry voices. They paused on the steps, listening.

"Just leave him alone, you two! He hasn't done anything to you!" It was a female voice, high with excitement.

"Oh, yes he has!" drawled a male voice. "He bothers me by just being here! I don't like his face!'

"Just stop it!" cried the female voice.

"It's Sarah!" exclaimed Dru and Brad together.

They shot up the stairs two at a time. When they rounded the corner, they saw Sarah standing angrily in the hall facing two boys: one white and the other black. Dru vaguely recognized the kids who hung around in the parking lot after school. They were trouble makers and drug dealers, but no one seemed to be able to do anything about them. They had free run of the parking lot, and if anyone complained about harassment, they found long, deep gashes in the finish of their car. Up to now, Brad and Dru had been able to avoid contact with them.

Standing between Sarah and the two thugs was a silent boy, who belonged to a group of Hispanic students who kept mainly to themselves. His shirt looked too big for his scrawny body, and his jeans were dirty and too short. He looked small and frightened, but his black eyes under straight, black hair looked defiant.

Brad took a deep breath, and though his heart was pounding, he forced himself to walk slowly toward the group, casually swinging his tennis racquet. Dru walked quietly beside him.

"Hye, Sarah!" he greeted her. "What's happening?" He spoke to Sarah, though his friendly grin included the three boys.

"Keep out of this, kid, if you know what's good for you," one of them growled. "You're another one who could go back where you came from." he added threateningly.

Brad casually dropped his tennis bag and lifted his tennis racquet and rested it on his right shoulder. "Yeah?" he said. "Now that doesn't seem too friendly. Why don't you and your little friend just run along and leave me and my friends alone?"

The Hispanic boy did not take his eyes off the two bullies, but he reached over and took Dru's racquet in his hand. He moved slightly to stand next to Brad and stood swinging the racquet back and forth beside his legs. They were smaller than the other two, but they were muscular and wiry. Dru noticed that the two bigger boys looked puffy and out of shape. They kept their eyes fixed on the tennis racquets.

For a long moment, nobody said a word. Then the two boys glanced at each other and shrugged. Together they turned and walked arrogantly down the hall. When they had gone a few steps, one of them turned slowly and spoke softly to the boy, but his voice carried perfectly in the enclosed corridor.

"Listen, Mex! You better watch out! Your nerdy friends don't play tennis every day, and nobody plays tennis at night!" They turned and sauntered down the hall, banging at the locker doors with their fists and laughing loudly.

They stood quietly in the corridor until the noise had faded away. The Hispanic student was the first to move. He handed Dru her racquet.

"Thanks," he said briefly, but he avoided

her eyes. He walked quickly off in the opposite direction.

Sarah watched him leave, tears in her eyes. "We've just made it worse for him," she said. "Now they're sure to find some way to get even. We made them look like fools; they'll take it out on him."

"Yeah!" agreed Brad. "If we'd left them alone, they might have just roughed him up some, but that would probably have been the end of it."

Sarah paused, then her blue eyes flashed. "No, we weren't wrong!" she declared angrily. "We can't let this sort of thing go on and simply ignore it. We have to take a stand sometime, and I'm doing it now!"

Brad looked at her in admiration. "I'm with you," he said, "but what's the problem? What did the kid do?"

"He didn't do anything," said Sarah. "It's because of what he is. He's one of the Mexican migrants who are spending the winter in Brannock County. You know how some people treat them! They work all summer for the farmers, picking tobacco and soybeans and other crops, but some of the farmers exploit them. They pay next to nothing, and whole families live in shacks without electricity or indoor plumbing. When winter comes, they haven't been able to save up enough money to go home. There's a group of them that live in a few run-down houses in a field south of town. They're in our school district, and that's why Eduardo is here. He's never been to school this long in one place before, but now those boys are going to make trouble for him. I can't let that happen!"

She turned around and walked to her locker.

"Wait, Sarah!" called Dru. "Aunt Kate is probably waiting outside. She'll be glad to give you a ride home."

"Thanks," said Sarah. She gave a weak smile through the tears that hung on her thick lashes.

Dru met Brad's eye as Sarah knelt at her locker. Both were worried, and in that silent communication that they sometimes shared, each could reach the other's thoughts. They couldn't help Sarah in her one woman campaign against injustice. The ghost wouldn't let them! He wouldn't allow them to rest until they had completed its mission, whatever it was. They simply didn't have time to get involved in Sarah's fight.

"Oh, well," Brad thought as he threw

Sarah's book bag over his shoulder. "If she gets involved in helping Eduardo and his friends, at least she'll be out of the ghost's way."

He put his arm around her waist and smiled into her eyes. He could smell the fresh scent of her hair.

Dru walked behind them watching as they spoke quietly, their faces close together. She had to beat down a sudden pang of resentment. It was tough having your best friend and your twin brother pairing off. Lately, they wanted to be alone, and although Dru was happy for them, she sometimes found it lonely.

They did make a good couple, though. Sarah was good for Brad. He had been in danger of getting a swelled head, and Sarah made him realize she didn't come easy. He was having to work for her.

She hoped Brad would be good for Sarah. She was so vulnerable. She was too much like Adalicia. They both felt things too deeply, and took on too many causes. For one fleeting second she had a flash of intuition, but it left as quickly as it had come.

## ANTIQUES

"Look at this!" Brad exclaimed excitedly. He held a wooden mallet in one hand. It was black with age and a large crack ran down the center of its handle.

"What's it worth, Aunt Kate?"

Dru looked at him and grinned. His hands were filthy. Grime covered his white tee shirt, and cobwebs clung to his jeans. Great black streaks ran across his face, just missing his eyes. He was perfectly happy!

"Be careful with that," she teased. "It's probably worth a hundred bucks."

"You think so?" asked Brad. He was serious. He laid it down reverently in a growing pile of broken and cracked objects.

Dru shook her head and turned away. Aunt Kate had propped a flashlight against a chair so the light shone into the gloom of an old cupboard. Dru could hear her clattering busily inside it, looking over objects forgotten for many years.

"There was no stopping the two of them," she thought. She sighed. Her heart just wasn't in this.

Suddenly Aunt Kate gave an exclamation of delight. "Come quickly!" she exclaimed excitedly. "Why, I had no idea! They're priceless!"

She was holding two iron kitchen implements in her hands, and even Brad and Dru could see that they were special. They had seen hundreds of clumsy pewter spoons and great iron meat forks that were used in kitchens long ago, and it was obvious the things Aunt Kate held in her hands were of superior workmanship.

One of them was a fork about fourteen inches long. Its slender handle was delicately twisted and topped by a smooth, round knob. It had two long, thin tines which were sharply tapered and ended in wicked points. When Brad took it in his hands, he could feel its superb balance.

The other implement was about the same length. Its handle was also twisted and ended in a knob, but its strange head was formed of several thin iron ropes which coiled and twisted back on themselves. It seemed impossible that the delicate iron loops and coils were the work of a nineteenth century blacksmith. Dru took it in her hands and turned it over, examining it.

"It's an egg whisk!" she exclaimed. "An egg whisk! It must have been made by a real artist."

"I do believe it was," said Aunt Kate slowly. She took the flashlight and pointed in into the cupboard. "There are other implements of the same quality in here, and they're unmistakably the work of old Quaker Ben!"

"Quaker Ben? Who was he?"

"He was an itinerant blacksmith who traveled around this part of the state before the Civil War. He converted a horse drawn cart into a forge, and he traveled from place to place. When he reached a town where he could get enough customers, he set up shop. He didn't shoe horses or do any other routine blacksmithing. The things he made were of high artistic quality like the ones here, and only the very wealthy could afford them. They're highly prized today, though they're so rare a museum is lucky to have even one."

"Wow!" exclaimed Brad reverently. He took

the whisk in his hands. "I bet it's worth a thousand bucks!"

"Oh, no you don't, young man!" cried Aunt Kate, taking the whisk from his hands. "These are not for sale. If they really are Quaker Ben's work, they're going straight to the State museum."

"But Aunt Kate," said Dru. "Why was he called 'Quaker Ben?' I didn't think the Quakers settled in this part of North Carolina."

"They didn't," said Aunt Kate. "Quaker Ben was from the North, Delaware or Pennsylvania, I believe. He was a mysterious figure in a way. The people around here became suspicious of him. They began to notice that every time he appeared in the neighborhood, another slave escaped. They suspected he was part of the underground railroad."

Dru's eyes glowed with interest. "That's right!" she exclaimed. "Quakers were strong abolitionists, and the Quakers in Delaware were an active group. They discovered a safe hiding hole in the basement of the governor's mansion in Dover a few years ago. It was a stop-over for the underground railroad."

Brad looked at her in amazement. "How do you know that!" he exclaimed.

"American History class last year."

"I was in that class, too, and I don't remember anything about that."

"Well, that doesn't surprise me. You and Aaron never listened to a thing Mrs. Shapiro said unless you thought you'd be tested on it."

"Yeah," Brad agreed. "She was boring."

Dru rolled her eyes. "Anyway," she said, her interest still high, "what happened to old Quaker Ben, Aunt Kate? Did they catch him?"

"Oh, no," said Aunt Kate. "He simply disappeared. I expect things got too hot for him here. I hope he managed to carry on his work in another part of the state, but we have no further record of him here in Brannock County.

Brad and Dru stood holding the implements and examining the fine workmanship. "Quaker Ben," Dru mused. In her mind's eye she could see him: dressed in black, long gray beard, sober but kindly face. "I wonder if Adalicia knew him?"

The afternoon passed quickly and before they realized it, the sun was throwing long shadows on the spring lawn.

"Goodness!" exclaimed Aunt Kate suddenly, glancing at her watch. "It's nearly 6:00. By the time we finish eating supper, it'll be dark. We'll have to put this off 'till tomorrow. When we work out here this summer, we can rig up an extension cord and get some light."

She stood with her hands on her hips. "Some folks around here never could get used to the fact that I installed electricity at Brannock Hall," she said darkly.

Brad and Dru exchanged amused glances behind her back. "Ida Lou," Brad mouthed silently.

Dru grinned. She believed Aunt Kate would rather find a ghost in her house any day than Ida Lou Duncan. She was still fuming over Ida Lou's plans for Brannock County Historical Day. She had suggested that Aunt Kate wear a colonial costume with farthingales and a mob cap and serve tea and lemon pound cake to the tourists. Aunt Kate asked her if she should also raise a goose and pluck its feathers for quill pens, but sarcasm was wasted on Ida Lou. She thought it was a "lovely idea Kate, honey, just a lovely idea!"

The thought of Ida Lou always threw Aunt Kate into a bad mood, and she stumped off to fix supper. Brad watched her walk away with affection.

"It's beginning to get dark," he said "and we haven't looked at the attic papers. Aunt

Kate expects us to work in here tomorrow. We can't tell her we'd rather work in the attic unless we tell her why."

"I know," said Dru, "but I'm glad we worked in here today. We needed a break, and it turned out to be fun. We'll just have to look at the papers tonight."

Brad leapt to his feet in alarm. "Tonight! Are you crazy! Night time is definitely not a good time to be alone in the attic!"

"Sure it is," she answered calmly. "We can just tell Aunt Kate we're tired and go upstairs right after supper. We can take flashlights with us. We'll have several hours."

"But," Brad babbled. "Do you really think that's a good idea? The door might get stuck again, or our flashlights might go out, or something."

Dru fixed him with a disgusted look. "Are you afraid?" she asked.

"Right!" he answered frankly.

"Well," she said, getting to her feet and brushing off the worst of the cobwebs. "You don't really have a choice. I'm going up there, and I know you won't let me go alone." She grinned at him over her shoulder as she opened the door.

"Oh, no!" Brad struck his forehead with

his hand and groaned. There was a knot forming in the pit of his stomach.

He made a feeble attempt to linger over dinner, but Dru was having none of that. She thrust a dish towel into his hands, and forced him to work at record speed. When they had finished, Brad followed her resignedly upstairs. They waited until the noises downstairs quieted, and they knew Aunt Kate was absorbed in the paper work she usually did after dinner.

Dru led the way to the attic. She tiptoed silently over the rough wooden floor boards, her flashlight cutting a weak path through the black attic air.

"Why don't we start on Jack LeFevre's letters?" she whispered. "We haven't looked at any of his yet."

"Why Jack LeFevre's?" hissed Brad. "He was only the overseer and wouldn't have known anything about Adalicia's private affairs," he added irritably. He was in no mood to be cooperative.

"I didn't have time to enlarge any of Adalicia's letters in the copy machine today," Dru whispered, "and we've already read a lot of Papa's. Before we read anymore, I'll need to enlarge them. We have to start somewhere, and we might as well read LeFevre's. They're nothing but account records and farm reports. We can tell by skimming them whether they're important or not. It probably won't take long."

"Okay," agreed Brad grudgingly. He hated it when Dru was being reasonable.

They knelt on the carpet and Dru opened the chest. It creaked loudly in the dark attic, and Brad jumped nervously. Dru reached in and removed the LeFevre letters.

"I've already arranged them by date," she told him. We'll start at the beginning, but we had better not risk the overhead light. Aunt Kate might see it and come up here to check. You hold the flashlight first and I'll read. We can switch in a little while."

The first letter was dated 1846 and contained a routine report on the plantation and its affairs. Lists of supplies and crops were of little interest to them, but Dru was struck with a thought.

"1846. That's the year Adalicia's mother died. Robert must have left home almost immediately. Adalicia was only two." She quickly leafed through the letters, checking the dates. There were only nine in 1846, but the next year there were twenty. The number increased each year until in 1861 there were forty-five.

"That's strange," Brad frowned thoughtfully. "LeFevre must have taken on more responsibility each year. By 1861 he must have thought he owned the place."

"It's really not so strange when you think about it," said Dru. "With Robert gone so much somebody had to take charge."

"Poor little girl!" said Brad angrily. "She might as well have not had a father."

"Yeah, if it weren't for Emily and Daniel, she wouldn't have had anybody. Listen to this!" Her eye had been caught by the mention of a familiar name.

*That black wench, Emily, is putting on airs. Not only does she live in the house like a white woman, but she is teaching herself to read. If you give me leave, sir, I'll whip a little sense back into her!*

Dru was horrified! "This letter is dated 1849. It's the same time she was beginning to read to Adalicia. She must have been teaching herself to read, too. The whole time she was working with Adalicia and loving her, Mr. LeFevre was writing ugly things to Papa."

"But Papa didn't pay any attention to him."

Brad spoke with more assurance then he felt. "He let Emily stay with her, and even let her have Daniel as a playmate."

Brad forgot all his earlier irritation. He handed Dru his flashlight, and excitedly took the stack of letters from her. He bent over them completely absorbed by the content. After weeks of studying the letters, the style and handwriting of the previous century had become familiar to them both, and they hardly noticed how swiftly there were able to read them now.

Brad skimmed each one. He stopped only when he found a mention of Adalicia or Emily or Daniel. Among the routine reports of crops and livestock, mention of Emily became more frequent and more hate filled, and in 1852 when Daniel entered Adalicia's life, LeFevre could scarcely contain his anger.

*The slave woman, Emily, has at last found a way to take her black brat out of my hands. She has introduced him into your household, Sir, as a playmate for your daughter, Adalicia. A likelier and stronger boy I never saw. He did bid fair to become a valuable field hand and, in-*

*deed, was already useful to me in a variety of ways, being quick and more intelligent than most.*

*Now, there he sits in your kitchen, eating your victuals and living as high as any gentleman's son. Unless you give me leave to put a stop to this, Sir, I cannot answer for the consequences.*

"Hurry!" hissed Dru. "Get out Papa's letters to LeFevre! Let's find the one near the same date and see what he answers."

Brad hurriedly opened the trunk and removed a stack of letters. He leafed through them until he located the letter dated two weeks after LeFevre's. It began with a remark on LeFevre's business dealings. With few exceptions, Papa okayed all his arrangements, thanking him for his thoroughness. He objected mildly to the breaking of another plot of ground for cotton,

*... for I fear the work is most strenuous, and I question whether or not it can be accomplished without use of the women and children. The work is hard for them. However, as*

*you are on the scene, you are the best judge. Do as you think best. I have no reason to doubt your management. As for that other matter concerning the slave boy, Daniel. Let it ride for the present. Adalicia likes him and he does no harm.*

"Good!" exclaimed Dru with satisfaction. "Papa might not have spent much time with Adalicia, but he loved her in his own way. He won't pay any attention to LeFevre and his lies and threats."

"I hope not," answered Brad. He covered a yawn with his hand. "Adalicia needs Daniel more than LeFevre does."

He glanced at his watch. "It's almost two o'clock!" he exclaimed in surprise.

"Listen to this," said Dru. She had picked up a letter dated October 1855. It was a report of the expenses and profits from the previous summer's crops. She scanned the columns of figures, and her orderly mind easily absorbed the information. "Even if Papa doesn't want to come home to check on Adalicia, he needs to come back and manage the plantation business. The farm is barely making a profit. He'll be ruined if something isn't done."

She paused for a minute, lost in thought. "LeFevre is growing tobacco and rice. Those were important crops before the Civil War, and should have brought in plenty! I wonder what he was doing wrong?"

Brad shrugged. He was exhausted and could hardly keep his eyes open. He stood up carefully, stretching his legs and back to relieve the cramping. "Put the letters away, Dru. I'm going to bed."

"Okay," agreed Dru reluctantly, but she was tired, too. "Maybe we can come up here tomorrow."

"Fine," mumbled Brad. All the affairs of one hundred and fifty years ago faded away from him in his need for sleep. Adalicia's blue eyes kept getting mixed up with Sarah's, and the laughter of the two girls seemed to tumble back and forth between the centuries until he couldn't tell them apart. Daniel, Emily, Quaker Ben, LeFevre, Papa: what had happened to all of them?

## LeFEVRE'S JOURNAL

Brad pushed his chair back from the table, and sighed unhappily. Sunlight flooded the spacious room and lay on the polished wood of Aunt Kate's mahogany table. It picked up the blues and reds from the fine old china and made it sparkle like jewels. It fell on the old Turkey carpet under their feet and lit up its faded colors until they, too, glowed dully.

Aunt Kate, always a good cook, outdid herself on Sundays. Brad looked at the crust fried chicken bones and remains of spoon bread on his plate. He had eaten almost nothing the night before, but made up for it today. Four pieces of chicken and two helpings of field peas and sweet potatoes was followed by two pieces of strawberry shortcake.

Brad looked expectantly at Aunt Kate.

"I do declare, Brad!" she said happily. "It

does a body good to see you eat so heartily."

"I knew you'd say that, Aunt Kate."

"How?" she asked in astonishment.

Because you always do!"

Aunt Kate snorted and Dru grinned in amusement.

"Well," said Brad, taking advantage of Dru's good humor. "I'll just head out to the old kitchen and get started while you two women do the dishes."

To his surprise, Dru only laughed, "Okay," she agreed, "but you owe me." She really didn't mind. She figured he went with her to the attic last night when he didn't want to, and she felt grateful.

Brad clattered hastily out the back door before she changed her mind and ran down the brick walk to the old kitchen. He pulled the latch on the heavy door and stood looking around him. They had hardly made a dent yesterday. In a cleared spot to the right of the door they had placed the few items they had examined and cleaned. Maybe he should carry them out to the storage area in the stable?

His eyes wandered around the room until they were caught by something in the back. Moving closer, he could just make out the outlines of a loft barely visible in the gloom.

With the help of his flashlight, he discovered it was built about six feet off the ground and extended along the entire width of the room. Somehow he had missed it yesterday. As his light played over one of the support poles, he noticed several deep gouges cut in the wood.

"They must be toe holds," he thought.

They turned the pole into a rough kind of ladder. Holding the flashlight in his teeth, he grasped the pole and, inserting his toes in the gouges, he easily climbed up. He shuddered a little as he brushed away sheets of cobwebs that clung softly to his face.

The loft was built too near the ceiling for him to stand, and he had to remain in a crouch while he flashed his light around. At first he was disappointed. The loft appeared empty. It was so dark up under the ceiling that even with a flashlight it was hard to see.

"It must have been a storage area," he thought. The cook probably let some of her kitchen helpers sleep up here on cold nights. The embers from the huge cooking fire would have kept the kitchen warm for hours. He was about to climb down when he flashed his light in the back and picked out something in one of the far corners.

Through the dust and cobwebs, he could

make out the shadowy form of a piece of furniture. Keeping his head low, and stumbling a little, he felt his way to it over the uneven planks. It was an old desk, sturdy and well built, but not fine enough to have been used in the main house. It was made of thick boards that had been roughly sanded and painted. It was probably used right here in the kitchen, he thought as he pulled the top drawer open and looked inside.

It was empty except for a book about ten inches square. He picked the book up and looked at it. It was filthy and it's leather cover was cracked and curled. The brittle pages inside were stained brown with moisture. He knocked the worst of the dust off against his knee, sneezing as some of it blew up his nose. When he opened the front cover, he gasped in astonishment! There was the same large, bold handwriting he and Dru had spent several hours studying the night before in the attic. It was still fresh in his memory.

He leafed quickly through the pages, skimming their contents. A few minutes was enough to convince him that he was holding the record book of the Brannock family plantation during the pre-war years. This was LeFevre's private journal. Some pages contained long columns of figures, but others were filled with closely written entries of daily life on the plantation.

Brad stood staring at his find. He could hardly believe his luck, and like Dru when she discovered Adalicia's portrait in the trunk, he wanted to examine it privately for a few minutes before he showed it to her.

He began to flip through it randomly. He was quickly sickened by LeFevre's violence! There were frequent accounts of brutal punishments handed out to the slaves. One horrible entry told of the attempted escape of two runaways. They had been hunted with dogs and captured after spending a night in the woods. LeFevre had them dragged back in chains and delayed their execution only long enough to gather the other slaves to watch them flogged. The mother of one of them was forced to be present!

Brad felt nauseated. His stomach was churning and cold beads of sweat were breaking out on his forehead. The feeling of distrust he and Dru had been developing toward LeFevre seemed mild now. The man was a monster! They had glimpsed only a hint of his cruel streak in the careful letters he had sent to Papa; but here in this private diary, he had allowed the full force of his nature to shine through. Brad threw the book on the desk and involuntarily stepped backward as though escaping from something evil.

Then struck by a thought, he picked it up again and began to leaf quickly through the pages, checking the dates. He soon found what he wanted. There in October 1855 was LeFevre's private account of the plantation profits. The figures he and Dru had seen the night before in LeFevre's letter to Papa were still fresh in his mind. It was just as he suspected! The accounts were wildly different. Rather than losing money, the crops from Brannock Hall were bringing in money, and lots of it! LeFevre was becoming a rich man by cheating Papa. Not that Brad cared about Robert Brannock, but LeFevre was also cheating Adalicia.

Brad stuck the book under his shirt and half crawled toward the ladder. Climbing down quickly, he walked to the door where the bright sunlight was spilling onto the floor. He leaned against the frame for support, and gulped in the fresh spring air. He felt heavy with depression. Events seemed reeling toward a conclusion that he was powerless to stop. At this moment Emily, Daniel and Adalicia seemed as real to him as Sarah, and Dru, and Aunt Kate.

He closed his eyes and could almost see Adalicia running toward him from behind the boxwood hedge, her arms full of sprays of yellow forsythia. She tossed a laughing remark over her shoulder to Daniel whose brown eyes sparked with fun. Emily was standing on the porch watching them, a gentle smile on her face, her arms folded calmly over her white apron.

He shook his head to clear the horror and dread which had been building in his mind for the past few months. He knew all along that something terrible must have happened to them. The three of them had been left in the hands of LeFevre, whose cruelty and hatred and dishonesty had been stronger than Adalicia's love and courage. The only protection they had was Papa. And Papa was weak!

He turned and headed for the house. He suddenly wanted to see Aunt Kate's kind face and hear Dru's laugh.

Later in the old parlor, the long silence was broken by Aunt Kate as she picked up her cup and sipped her tea. She looked around the room with its fine old antiques. Her eyes swept past Colonel Brannock's walnut desk and out the tall, double doors. They were standing open to allow the fragrant spring air to flow in from the veranda.

"To think," she said softly, "that all that happened right here." She looked at the journal Brad held in his hands. They had been reading it for the last hour, ever since Brad returned from the old kitchen. They had just finished reading the account of the hanging of the runaways, and were stunned into temporary silence.

"It's funny," thought Dru, "how the past and the present keep getting mixed up in this old house. I wonder if Adalicia seems real to us because we know she sat in this room, maybe on this very sofa, and drank her tea from the cup Aunt Kate is holding. Aunt Kate never cared much about Adalicia. When she looks at this room, she probably sees Colonel Brannock sitting at his desk with baby Robert playing at his feet."

She took a deep breath, "Aunt Kate," she said. "What do you know about LeFevre? What happened to him?"

Aunt Kate thought for a moment. "I don't really know much about that period. The early history of Brannock Hall, when people like the Colonel were developing the new United States, always seemed much more interesting to me. I never cared much about Robert Brannock. He married Adalicia's beautiful young mother when he was almost fifty, and when she died only three years later, he spent most of his time away from home dabbling in pre-war politics, but he was never very important. He never became the leader his father had been, and he was killed in one of the early skirmishes."

She glanced at LeFevre's book. "Nobody has ever been able to understand why Brannock Hall declined so quickly during Robert's time. It would have taken a fool to fail. But now we know why," she said bitterly. "Someday soon I've got to start on the papers in the third trunk. It probably holds the answers to several puzzling questions. I always wondered why Brannock Hall wasn't burned by Yankee troops during the last days of the war when so many other great homes were. Mama thought it was because the Yankees had used Brannock Hall as their military headquarters, but I wondered why they didn't burn it whey they left." She sat, her hands folded in her lap, lost in thought.

"Weren't you ever curious about Adalicia?" asked Dru.

"Well," Aunt Kate hesitated. There was a

worried frown between her eyebrows. "Every family has a person they don't like to talk about. In our family Adalicia was one of those people. I grew up believing that there was some mysterious thing she had done that brought shame on the family. I always accepted that without giving it much thought, and never cared enough to find out; but this changes everything." She gestured toward LeFevre's journal. "There seem to be too many lies. Maybe there were lies about Adalicia, too. She was only two years older than you when she died, Dru."

"Well," she said, getting to her feet. "The answer is probably in the papers in the third trunk. Someday soon I'll have to start on them. I know you haven't had time, what with school work and tennis practice and everything else. Maybe we can work on them this summer."

Dru caught Brad's eye. Reprieve! They both knew Aunt Kate was too excited about her antique hunt in the old kitchen to be sidetracked by the papers in the trunk. By this summer they'd have already found the answer. The ghost would see to that! He was unusually quiet lately, but only because he knew they were working hard. They had a feeling he would not be patient much longer.

## PLOTS

Dru set her orange juice on the table with a clatter and looked in surprise at the back door. A figure had appeared on the porch and was standing quietly in the shadows.

"Sarah!" she exclaimed.

She glanced worriedly at Brad. They had been successful in keeping Sarah away from Brannock Hall and the ghost until now.

Sarah opened the door slowly and walked into the sunny kitchen. She looked beautiful as usual. Her long, dark hair fell in masses of shining curls down her back, and she was wearing a blue leather mini skirt which showed off her slender legs. But there were deep, ugly circles around her eyes.

"Sarah! Are you sick?" asked Dru in concern. She pushed her chair back from the table and slipped her arm around Sarah's waist.

Sarah shook her head, but there were tears in her eyes. "No," she said. "I'm not sick, but something terrible has happened! I wanted to call you last night and tell you about it, but I was too depressed." She looked at Brad.

"Here!" interrupted Aunt Kate. She pushed Sarah into a chair and placed a hot, buttered biscuit and a steaming cup of sweetened tea in front of her. Sarah smiled slightly, but shook her head.

"Drink the tea, anyhow," urged Aunt Kate. "It always helps."

Sarah picked up the cup and took several sips. They watched her anxiously.

"It happened yesterday," she said. "I was late coming home from cheerleading practice. When I got there, nobody else was home. I was having a snack and watching TV when I heard tires squealing and horns blowing outside. I ran to the window, and I saw two carloads of boys, wearing Halloween masks. They drove off the street, right onto our front lawn. Some of them threw eggs against the windows, and they took cans of paint and sprayed words on the front of our house. I didn't think they knew I was inside at first, but just as they were leaving, one of them saw me at the window. He pointed me out to the others, and they all began laughing and shouting things at me. I pulled the shade down and ran around locking the doors. Then I ran to my room and cried."

Dru glanced at Brad. She had never seen him so angry.

"I don't know how long it was before Mom came home, but she was furious and called the sheriff. The sheriff and his men stayed a long time and took a lot of pictures. I just wanted to be left alone, but they kept asking me questions. They didn't believe I couldn't help them! The boys were all wearing masks and it was impossible to know who they were."

Sarah put her head down on the table and her shoulders shook as she broke into tears. Dru and Aunt Kate stood anxiously behind her, patting her back and making soothing noises. Brad sat silently at his seat watching them. There was an angry scowl on his face.

"Oh, Dru!" sobbed Sarah. "Nothing like this has ever happened to me before, and I've lived here all my life. The boys seemed so full of hate, and the sheriff's men made me feel worse. They thought I had done something to deserve all this. They made me feel I was to blame, and the things the boys wrote on our house were true!"

She took a tissue from Dru and dried her eyes. "There was one of them, Deputy Travers, who finally made them stop. He saw how upset they were making me, and he told me to go upstairs. He made them leave me alone."

"Randy Travers," exclaimed Aunt Kate. She looked pleased.

Brad and Dru remembered the traffic ticket Aunt Kate had gotten from Mr. Travers in the winter. She was right about him. He was a nice guy.

"Mom is going to the high school to see Mr. Anderson today. Dad wanted to drive me to school, but I persuaded him to let me ride the bus. I wanted to tell you and Miss Kate what happened." She looked at Brad.

"Come on upstairs," Dru said. "We have time to fix your make-up before the bus comes."

"Sarah!" Brad's voice was still angry. "What did they write on your house?"

She hesitated a moment, and almost refused to answer, but then she looked into his angry, brown eyes and something in them made her blush a little.

"They called me a 'Mex lover' and painted a few Nazi swastikas, but the worst were a lot of filthy words that boys like that always call girls. Dad was phoning the painters when I left. I hope it's covered before I get home from school. It makes me feel cheap and dirty!"

Brad moved restlessly around the room, picking up objects and replacing them on the shelves. "This must have something to do with Eduardo," he said. "I've seen you eating lunch with him and his friends a couple of times."

"I think so, too," she answered. "After what happened in the hall the other day, I decided to try to get to know him better. I asked if I could sit with him and practice my Spanish. I don't think he trusted me at first, but lately we've been getting along a lot better. Eduardo plays the guitar, and he's very good! He even wrote a Spanish song about me and the other cheerleaders. Something about short skirts and flamingos. I don't understand all of it and he says it can't be translated exactly. I think it pleased him that I could take a joke. I found out that Maria, his girlfriend, is one of Mr. Carpenter's advanced art students, and I've been thinking about asking her and Eduardo to serve on the May dance committee. I thought we might even have a Mexican theme with pinatas. Everybody likes Mexican food!"

She sat for a moment with her head in her hands. "But this changes everything," she said in a muffled voice. She began to cry again. "When I left the house this morning, I felt like the words on the walls were screaming at me. I could hear them all the way down the road. I don't think I've ever felt so bad before in all my life!"

She scraped her chair back from the table and dejectedly followed Dru up the stairs. Brad looked after her sadly. He didn't like to see her like this. She looked defeated, as though the bigots and the liars had won.

Somehow the news of what happened at Sarah's house spread like wildfire through the school. Fortunately, most of the students knew Sarah too well to believe anything bad about her, but there was enough whispering and giggling to make Brad angry. Several times during the day Dru had seen them together in the hall with his arm thrown protectively around her shoulders.

Dru let him handle it. She was more worried about Adalicia. She was reaching the end of the letters, and had a strange feeling she was racing against some imaginary clock. She planned to spend the afternoon in the attic, and found it hard to concentrate on anything else.

The sunlight was fading from the attic

when Dru looked up from the letter she was holding and rubbed her tired eyes. She glanced around at the stacks of yellowed papers arranged neatly about her on the floor, and a worried crease appeared between her eyes. She sat lost in thought. Somehow this was all too real. Adalicia told her story too well. She seemed almost alive to Dru, and sometimes when she placed the stacks of papers back in the trunk for safekeeping, she had a feeling she was stuffing Adalicia, herself, into the darkness - prying her hands loose from the sides and closing the lid on her face.

She stood up suddenly and shook herself. "Don't be silly!" she told herself sharply. "They're just pieces of paper. Adalicia's been dead for over one hundred years."

Frowning slightly, she glanced at her watch. Brad must still be with Sarah. She could have used him this afternoon. She sensed that there was not much time left to discover Adalicia's secret. Brannock Hall was nervous! There was a feeling in the air: a restlessness that was growing stronger. Even Aunt Kate seemed on edge at times, and Dru did not like the tension. Most of the tricks had stopped. They no longer found their light cords cut or their clothes slung around, but somehow that only made things worse. The tricks had been so childish, they almost seemed like practical jokes. She knew Brad was terrified of whatever was in the house, but she was never able to take it as seriously. How can you be afraid of a ghost that has a sense of humor no matter how revolting? But now, she was becoming more afraid even as Brad was relaxing a little.

There was a sort of vibration in the house. It was waiting! And it was growing impatient! There were sharp, excited knocks. Little angry wisps of air, and low moaning noises came through the hole at night. She felt a strength and an anger building that she knew they wouldn't be able to control. Time was growing short. She needed Brad now! They ought to devote all their spare time to the mystery. If only Sarah's problems didn't distract him too much! They'd both be able to help Sarah full time as soon as they satisfied the ghost.

She didn't like what she learned this afternoon from the letters. Aunt Sarah, whom Adalicia had expected to love with all her heart, was quickly becoming her worst enemy; and to make matters worse, she seemed to be forming some sort of alliance with LeFevre. She was one of those people who feel all young people are wicked and need to be disciplined, and she was suspicious of Adalicia. Her letters to Papa were full of criticism of Adalicia's "headstrong ways" which she blamed on the influence of Emily and Daniel. She hated the gentle Emily especially, and felt everything she disapproved of must be her fault.

"The old bag!" Dru thought angrily. "I don't understand how Papa can listen to this stuff for one minute."

Emily, who had spent years loving and teaching Adalicia, was banished to the kitchen where she was forced to lift and scour the heavy iron pots in the intolerable heat. She was small and fragile and not used to such heavy work. She quickly became ill, and Adalicia wrote pleading letters to her father begging him to release her from her kitchen duties.

Though LeFevre was smart enough not to criticize Adalicia to her father, his letters contained frequent hints about the laziness of the household before "Miss Sarah's" arrival, and oily compliments about her.

Daniel had been banished from the house completely and neither Adalicia nor Emily were allowed to see him. He worked from sun up to sun down with the other field hands.

Daniel was young and strong and the field work was not hard for him physically, but his years with Emily and Adalicia had not only educated him, but had also taught him gentlemanly manners and given him a bearing which was straight and proud. LeFevre thought he was "uppity" and hated him, and was determined to break his spirit. Frequently, he was whipped or humiliated in some other way. Though Emily suffered horribly in the kitchen, Daniel perhaps suffered more, despite his youth and strength. Aunt Sarah was content to coldly ignore Emily as long as she stayed out of the way and did her work.

In one letter Adalicia told her father of finding Daniel lying unconscious on the dirt floor of one of the sheds, his back bleeding from crisscrossed lashes. She had cleaned his wounds and secretly nursed him for several days, but was afraid to bring him to the house for fear of involving Emily. This letter, at least, had brought some action on Papa's part. A healthy young slave was worth a lot of money in those days, and he wrote a stern letter to LeFevre forbidding him to maim Daniel because he was valuable property.

Dru frowned. Daniel meant no more to Papa than a good horse. To him, Daniel was not a human being – he was an investment.

The letters from Adalicia to her father were sad now. Robert had not been home since Aunt Sarah's arrival, but even so, Adalicia had not lost faith in "dearest Papa." It seemed to Dru that Adalicia still felt if she could make her father understand how things really were, he would put everything to rights again.

Dru sighed. She wished she could reach back through the years and warn Adalicia what Aunt Sarah and LeFevre were saying about her in their letters. Though Aunt Sarah was the sort of person who prided herself on never telling a lie, and wrote what was only the strictest truth, she disliked Adalicia so much that she could find nothing but critical things to say about her while pretending to be concerned for her welfare.

Jack LeFevre's letters, on the other hand, were full of hatred, and contained barefaced lies about almost everything and everybody except Adalicia. He seemed to sense that although Robert paid almost no attention to Adalicia, he would not tolerate criticism of her from his overseer. This made what he wrote about her in his private journal even worse. Somehow his hypocrisy was worse than his lies. Adalicia was standing alone, fighting for two weak people who loved her against two strong people who hated her.

"This is bad," thought Dru. "Adalicia is too strong to take this much longer. Something is bound to happen soon." She looked at the dwindling pile of letters. Adalicia was fifteen now.

She spoke aloud, "This week!" she said. "We should find out what happened this week!"

She returned the letters to the trunk and went downstairs. As she entered the kitchen, Brad clattered up the porch and into the door. He threw his tennis racquet on the counter and took a biscuit from the basket Aunt Kate was carrying to the table.

"Oh, good!" Dru greeted him. "You're home and we can eat. Take your racquet off the counter."

Brad obligingly took the racquet off the counter and absent-mindedly set it on the table. He walked over to the sink and began to wash his hands. Dru sighed and placed the tennis racquet on the floor beside the steps where he would see it. She watched in disgust as he finished washing his hands and stood with water dripping on Aunt Kate's clean floor looking vaguely around for a towel.

Before she could offer him the one she was holding, he wiped his hands on his jeans and moved over to inspect the food on the table.

"Great!" he exclaimed. "Country ham and biscuits. You didn't put any okra in the grits, did you, Aunt Kate?"

"Okra in the grits!" she exclaimed. "What on earth for?"

Brad grinned. "Just checking. You put okra in just about everything else."

Aunt Kate merely snorted.

There was silence as they heaped their plates and ate. Dru glanced at Brad and Aunt Kate. Both were unusually quiet. Brad was already devouring a second biscuit without seeming to taste what he was cramming into his mouth. Aunt Kate, who usually had a hearty appetite, was picking at her food. Brad broke the silence first.

"Aunt Kate, what do you know about the migrant workers in Brannock County? Back home we live in the city, and we don't know anything about the farming business."

Aunt Kate sighed. "I don't know as much about them as I should, and what I do know is not always pleasant. A lot of farmers in this part of the state need help almost all summer harvesting their crops. There are families of people, many from Mexico and Puerto Rico, who travel from place to place trying to find work as crop pickers. They start with spring crops like strawberries, and work through the summer in soybeans and tobacco.

"A few dishonest farmers pay them less than minimum wages because many of them are illegal aliens and are afraid to report abuses for fear they'll be sent back home where they can't find jobs. Whole families, including children, work in the fields. The farmers are required by law to provide housing, but the dishonest ones provide dreadful houses and charge high rents. Some of them even own the nearest grocery store, and they charge such high prices for the food that the workers have to go into debt to pay their grocery bills. Of course, the farmer is the one the workers owe the money to! By the end of the summer, the farmer owns almost everything the workers have, and they don't have enough money saved to move away. They have to stay and keep on working to pay off their debts. In the end, they become almost like slaves."

Brad looked at her steadily for a moment. "Sarah wonders how people in this county can let something like that happen."

Aunt Kate sighed and pushed her plate

away. "I don't know, Brad. I suppose its easier to study the problems of our ancestors than to face the ones we have today. Now, you two run along and get your homework done. It's late, and I'll do the dishes. I need time to think."

Brad and Dru willingly clattered up the steps.

"Brad," Dru spoke through the hole, "how is Sarah? What did you find out today?"

"I don't know. She's not very happy, and something is going on. Eduardo and his girl-friend weren't at school, and the parking lot crowd was hanging around after class. I saw Sarah's father in Mr. Anderson's office. He drove us both home. That's why we weren't on the bus. I hung out with Sarah for a while, but I don't think her father liked it. So I came on home. He's going to drive her to school tomorrow."

"Did he get the house painted before she came home?

"Most of the front, but you can still see some stuff through the first coat of paint. People keep driving by the house to stare."

There was a few moments silence while they settled on their beds with their homework. Dru could hear Brad opening his book bag.

"What did you find out about Adalicia?" Brad asked.

"Well," she answered. "It doesn't look good. I'd like to reach back in time and shake some sense into Adalicia's father. It's hard to imagine that he could be the son of the Colonel. You'd think he would've inherited a little backbone. If it's not Jack LeFevre writing lies to him, it's that old witch, Aunt Sarah. I don't know which one's the worst. LeFevre was wicked and dishonest, but at least we know where he stood. Aunt Sarah pretended to love Adalicia, but I believe she hated her as much as LeFevre did."

"But why? Have you been able to figure out why they hated her?"

"I'm not sure about LeFevre yet, but I think I know why Aunt Sarah hated her. I believe she hated almost everybody. Do you remember Mrs. Eberly who used to live next door to us? Remember how she used to stand on her porch and yell at us if we skated past her house?"

"Sure," answered Brad. "Mom used to tell us she was lonely and we had to be polite to her, but I was afraid of her. I was only five. I was afraid she might catch me and eat me for lunch!"

"Anyhow," Dru continued. "I think Aunt Sarah must have been just like Mrs. Eberly. She was unhappy and she wanted to blame somebody for her problems. She hated Adalicia because she was young and beautiful. She was jealous."

"Listen to this!" She picked up a letter.

*My Dear Robert,*

*I feel it is my Christian duty to warn you of Adalicia's wild behavior before it is too late and she brings shame upon us all. The influence she long received at the hands of black Emily is still showing in her manners. She pays no attention to my advice, and actually prefers the company of that low woman to mine, her only aunt, who has the tenderest concern for her welfare. Last night I found her in the kitchen. Her flowered muslin gown was full of cinders and her hands were covered with black grease from scouring the cooking pots.*

*Fancy! Your own daughter, the mistress of Brannock Hall, laboring like a common slave! When I insisted she return immediately to the house and leave Emily to her work, she hotly refused, making excuses for Emily, whom she said was ill.*

*And now, dear brother, it pains me to add further to your knowledge of Adalicia's character. That good Mr. LeFevre, on whom we both depend, most kindly informed me that Adalicia sometimes leaves the house late at night and brings food to the shed which he uses as a jail for slaves, such as Daniel, who seem to respond to no other punishment. Mr. LeFevre would, of course, never allow Daniel to starve, for he is your property and a valuable field hand, but a day or two without food brings him under control as nothing else can. Adalicia is wild and headstrong, and was allowed to run unchecked too long with slaves and other riffraff.*

*However distressed you may be at these tidings of your only daughter, there is worse to come. Brace yourself, my dear Robert, for what can only cause you deeper pain.*

"What!" exclaimed Brad. "What other horrible thing can she have done besides helping a sick woman and feeding a starving man!"

"Sh-h-h-h!" hissed Dru. "Aunt Kate will hear you!"

*She was seen Wednesday night last, leaving the grounds on her pony, Rainbow. She was followed, and was seen to enter the woods where she met a young man who was waiting for her there. A sudden noise frightened him, and he fled before he could be apprehended. Despite my pleas, she admits to no wrongdoing, but you may rest assured, my dear Robert, that I will do everything in my power to discover the name of the villain who is involved with Adalicia in this new wickedness. Meanwhile, she is confined to the house. I shall never relax as long as I am her guardian! It pains me to add this burden to your shoulders already bowed down with responsibilities. You may depend on LeFevre and me to attend with devoted attention to your affairs here at Brannock Hall.*

Dru threw the letter down with disgust.

"She ends with the usual stuff about her Christian duty, and Adalicia's ungratefulness."

"What!" Brad's voice carried loudly through the hole. "So she sneaked out and met her boyfriend! So what! What's the big deal? Aunt Sarah can put her on probation, take her off knitting or something. Plenty of girls have done worse."

"Not in the nineteenth century, stupid!" answered Dru. "Things were different then. Girls were strictly chaperoned. I can't believe Adalicia would have broken the rules like that. Helping Emily and Daniel was one thing, but meeting boys in the woods was something else. It just wasn't done! It would have ruined Adalicia's reputation and would have thrown the whole family into disgrace. People in the neighborhood would have whispered and gossiped and would have quit speaking to them or inviting them to their houses. Adalicia may have been headstrong, but she wasn't foolish. I wonder who he was?"

"It must have been another one of Aunt Sarah's lies!" exclaimed Brad hotly. He was unwilling to believe anything negative about Adalicia. Her blue eyes were too much like Sarah's.

"I don't think so," answered Dru slowly.

"Aunt Sarah didn't lie. Just because she only reported bad things doesn't make any difference. The things she did report were always true. If she said Adalicia met a man in the woods, she probably did!"

"Well," asked Brad, his interest aroused, "who was he?"

Dru was quiet for a moment. "Maybe she did find a lover," she mused. "He must have been dashing, and handsome, and rich, and slightly mysterious: someone Aunt Sarah would never have approved of."

"Give me a break! Rhett Butler lived in Atlanta, not Brannock County!" Brad said in disgust.

"You know!" Dru was suddenly struck with another thought. "Someone must have spied on Adalicia. They were watching her every move, even at night. How else would Aunt Sarah have known Adalicia was out on her pony?"

"You're right! It must be LeFevre. It couldn't have been anybody else."

Dru could hear is bed creak as he jumped to the floor. "Let's get LeFevre's journal from the parlor and read some more. I can't stand the suspense!"

They tiptoed quietly down the back steps,

checking in the kitchen to see if Aunt Kate was still there.

"She's not here," whispered Dru. "I wonder where she is?"

"I don't know," answered Brad, but she's not in the parlor either."

He took the journal from Aunt Kate's desk and sat down on the sofa. "We can read in here."

Dru sat down beside him and looked around. The lamps on either side of the sofa shone with a mellow glow. They looked soft, like candle light. She always felt closest to Adalicia in this room, probably because it had remained most like it was in 1850 than any other room in the house.

"Here's the entry for that week," Brad was saying. He leaned closer to the lamp, holding the journal directly under its glow.

> *The girl is nearing the breaking point. She cannot long endure Daniel's suffering. I have kept him under lock and key and on starvation rations for a week, now. She is headstrong and impatient. She will do something foolish, and when she does, I'll be ready!"*

"What a jerk!" exclaimed Brad angrily.

"Go on!" said Dru eagerly.

"There's an entry almost every day that week. I'll skip over the routine farm business. There was a long silence as he skimmed the yellowed pages.

"His handwriting is getting harder to read," he said. It's much sloppier than it was in the early entries. It's taking longer to decipher."

"Let me see," said Dru with interest. She took the book from Brad's hands.

"You're right!" she said after a brief inspection. "His writing is getting larger and looser and there are huge ink blotches all over the pages. Look at his 'e's!' The ones in this entry look more like 'l's,' and he's forgetting to cross his 't's.'"

"Yep! He's losing it!" declared Brad, leaning back and crossing his arms over his chest.

"Oh, great!" exclaimed Dru. "He's not only a liar and a cheat, but now he's a psychopath, too."

"Give it back!" said Brad reaching for the journal. "Let's find out what happened."

*Wednesday*
*I have taken the precaution of*
*posting the slaves, Tom and Wilson,*

*outside her windows at night. She is
so carefully watched by that ugly old
fool, Miss Brannock, during the day,
that she can take no action. But the
wench is stupid enough to think she
can act safely under the cover of darkness. She feels every slave on the plantation loves her and would never spy
on her. The wealthy always forget
what a little money will make a poor
man do. Tom will follow her if she
leaves, and Wilson will waken me.
They have been paid, and it will not
go well for them if they disobey my
instructions.*

*Thursday*

*The foolish wench has taken the
bit in her mouth, as I knew she would.
Last night she left the house around
mid-night. She saddled Rainbow, and
was off! Tom followed her as best he
could by foot, but that scoundrel,
Wilson, claimed he got lost in the
darkness and could not find his way
to my dwelling until she had time to
make good her escape. Tom prances
around with the jingle of my coins in*

his pocket, but Wilson was given a reward of a different kind. He cannot prance at all! I fancy he will make a more reliable watchman in the future.

Friday

She has tried it again! This time I was saddled and waiting for her as soon as the warning was given. I followed her to the little stand of silver birches on the north side of the property. At one time I feared I had lost her, but I glimpsed the silk lining of her cloak gleaming in the moonlight. I dared not follow her into the woods, for fear of being seen, but I now know how to lay my plans in the future.

I shall hide Tom and Wilson there and we shall soon discover what business the lass has in those woods so late at night. I fancy she is meeting someone who will not please her father. First I must determine who he is, and then I must decide what use I can make of my knowledge. I am much mistaken if I cannot turn this to my advantage.

*Saturday*
*I have her! I now know the name of the scoundrel she's been scheming with in the woods.*

*She can keep no secrets from Jacque LeFevre. The lass has walked into my snare, and I can't answer for the consequences.*

*But it is too dangerous. I can no longer record in this journal. What happens from now on is locked in secrecy, for the stakes are too high. But you may rest assured that I hold all the aces, and that everyone, even that weak fool Robert Brannock, will have to reckon with Jacque LeFevre from now on.*

Brad hurriedly turned the rest of the pages. "That's all!" he exclaimed. "There is no more!"

"But what happened?" asked Dru in alarm. "There's something terribly wicked here. Adalicia is walking straight into his trap."

Brad sat staring at the journal. When he spoke, his voice was thoughtful. "Dru, I wonder if it's possible the man she's been meeting could be old Quaker Ben? We know

Quaker Ben was an abolitionist and we know he was here because we found his tools in the old kitchen. Surely Adalicia would have contacted him about saving Daniel and Emily! That would explain LeFevre's excitement. It's hard to believe she could be meeting a lover while Daniel and Emily are in so much trouble."

"You're right," agreed Dru. "Her letters to Papa are so sad. They don't sound like a woman in love."

Brad rolled his eyes.

"They don't, Brad! It's like she can't think of anything else but Daniel and Emily. Your idea about Quaker Ben makes sense. She's probably been meeting him to arrange Daniel and Emily's escape and LeFevre knows about it. She's in terrible danger! LeFevre can destroy them all."

They sat silently in the peaceful little parlor. The pools of light from the lamps reflected off the polished floor and onto their worried faces. Suddenly the massive old grandfather clock, which had stood for two centuries in the entrance hall, began to chime. Slowly it struck twelve times while they sat unmoving.

Just as it finished, the front door opened, and in walked Aunt Kate with her usual briskness. They looked at her in surprise.

"Where have you been, Aunt Kate?" asked Dru.

"I've been to see Ida Lou Duncan," she answered firmly.

"Ida Lou!" they spoke in unison. They were too shocked to say anything else. The news almost drove thoughts of Adalicia out of their minds. They would have been less surprised if Aunt Kate left the house at midnight to meet Jacque LeFevre!

"Yes," she said. "Ida Lou's a foolish woman in many ways, but if you want to get something done, she's the one to see. Now, I'm locking up down here, and you two look as though you could use some sleep."

They were too dispirited to argue. Both dragged off to bed. There was nothing any one of them could do for Adalicia now, not even Ida Lou.

# 13

## ADALICIA ELOPES

*Dear Papa,*

*I cannot tell you with what pain I write. Prepare yourself for the worst, my father, for what you are about to read will grieve you. I can but hope that after the first shock has worn away, the love you have always held for me will soften your heart. I can assure you that only the gravest circumstances would force me to take the action I am about to describe to you.*

*You have known for quite some time of my unhappiness, but were it only my own welfare at stake, I would gladly bear any burden to keep from causing you pain. However, another is involved in my decision. In short,* my dear father, I am eloping with a man whom I love and who loves me in return, though I cannot tell you his name.

I find I am no longer able in good conscience to live at Brannock Hall. The place I loved as a child has become one I hate as a woman. The enslavement of human beings is a practice I can no longer tolerate.

I am off, dearest Papa. I believe our nation stands at the brink of a terrible war with one section divided against the other. The two of us must be divided also, for I find I must align myself against the very cause you have worked for. It may be many years, if ever, before we meet again. When I am safely away and settled, I shall try to send you my address, if that is still possible. May I hope to hear from you?

In closing, let me assure you again and again that I would not take so important a step - and one that I know will cause you so much pain - did I not feel there were no other course. I leave your house asking *nothing from you except your love. I take nothing belonging to you with me other than that which you have already most generously bestowed upon me.*

> *Always your loving daughter,*
> *Adalicia Brannock*

Brad's voice trailed away. He sat staring at the letter in his hands. Dru sat opposite him, shocked into silence!

"I can't believe it!" cried Brad. "She was meeting a lover in the woods! And now she's going to sneak away with him. Aunt Sarah was right about her. It wasn't Quaker Ben after all. All those fancy words don't mean a thing. She's going to run away. She's going to desert Emily and Daniel!"

"It doesn't seem like Adalicia," Dru spoke quietly.

Brad gave a short, angry laugh. He felt betrayed. "She's running away! She's abandoning Emily and Daniel and taking off with some drifter she's been meeting in the woods. She's not thinking about anybody but herself."

Dru looked at him curiously. "What makes you think he was a drifter, Brad?"

"There's no other logical explanation. If

he was the son of someone they all knew, she would've met him openly in the house. Even if Aunt Sarah had disapproved, Adalicia would've brought him to the house anyhow. She wasn't afraid of Aunt Sarah, and she was the mistress of Brannock Hall. There must've been something really wrong with him. Something she was trying to hide."

Dru nodded. This was the last thing she would have expected Adalicia to do. "Maybe she planned to take Emily and Daniel with her. Just because she was getting married, doesn't mean she had to leave them behind."

"I don't think so. She made a point of telling her father she wasn't taking anything that belonged to him, and Emily and Daniel belonged to her father. Besides, she's obviously not eloping with Quaker Ben, and he's the only one who could have helped her smuggle Emily and Daniel out of the county."

"It does look bad," Dru admitted. Despite what she wrote to her father about her conscience, it did seem as though she were deserting Emily and Daniel and leaving everything in LeFevre's hands; and all for someone she could hardly have known.

She spoke thoughtfully. "Maybe we have it figured wrong, Brad. Maybe her boyfriend was also an abolitionist. Quaker Ben might not've been the only person who could help her."

Brad picked up Adalicia's letter and quickly re-read it. "I don't think so, Dru. I don't know much about Civil War history, but it seems to me that two abolitionists working in a county this small would have been impossible, and she couldn't have gotten very far with two runaway slaves unless someone with a lot of experience was helping her. Emily and Daniel were her father's slaves. They were his property. In the end, she couldn't get over that. I guess she was a victim of her upbringing. She didn't like it, but the only thing she could think to do was run away."

"Well, anyhow, that's the last letter!" Brad threw it down in disgust. "She left and went away, and for all we know, she lived happily ever after."

He clattered down the steps. "I've got to hurry. I'm meeting Sarah before classes."

Dru remained sitting on the floor, her eyes staring at the letter lying on the carpet. She reached out and touched it. It made her feel sad, almost as though Adalicia were lying there, discarded and helpless.

Suddenly she stiffened. How could they have forgotten! Adalicia couldn't have left

Brannock Hall! Her grave was in the slave cemetery. She died when she was sixteen!

That's almost now, Dru thought. Something happened soon after she wrote that last letter, and whatever it was caused her father to desert her and bury her in the slave cemetery. Surely, even in those days, a daughter wouldn't have been treated that harshly just because she eloped. In fact, it was difficult to believe Robert really cared. He didn't care about anything else she did. There must be something else.

Bells were ringing in her head! They still didn't know the answer. Whatever Adalicia had planned was more than an elopement, and it surely involved Emily and Daniel even if Quaker Ben wasn't involved. Dru almost laughed aloud in relief; but there were no other letters, no other papers, no other journals. Nothing else. How could she find out? One thing she knew. She couldn't abandon Adalicia or lose faith in her. There was something she was supposed to discover, and whatever it was, was a piece of history. The facts had to be recorded somewhere. Adalicia was the mistress of Brannock Hall, and her death couldn't have been hushed up.

Dru glanced at her watch and jumped up.

She had just enough time to make it to the bus stop. Maybe she'd be able to come up with a plan during the day.

Her classes passed in a blur, one dragging behind the other until last period finally arrived. Dru with her book propped open on her desk, and her head lowered. Her left arm lay across her lap, partially hidden by her jacket. Her eyes were fixed on the second hand of her watch. Suddenly the air was torn by the ear splitting buzz of the dismissal bell.

Instantaneously there was the clap of twenty-five geometry books slapping shut. It was important to time it just right! Mr. Abbott gave a detention slip to anyone who closed his book before the bell rang.

She quickly stuffed her papers into her bag, and was the first one out the door. She had only a few seconds to beat the rush in the hall, and she needed to hurry. Quickly she ran up the steps to the second floor. She ducked into the library just as a wave of noisy students took over the hall. She stood inside the door, breathing heavily.

Mrs. Hamilton looked up in surprise. "Why, Dru," she exclaimed. "What can I do for you?"

Hurriedly, Dru explained what she

wanted. "Is there someplace I can look at old newspapers printed in Brannock County?"

"Of course, Dru. You already know that. The Free Press is filed for two weeks beneath the periodical rack in the media center. The back copies from 1985-1991 are bound and are on the shelves."

"No. I mean really old - like about 1860."

"Oh," said Mrs. Hamilton. "You want to see the historical newspapers. We don't have those here, of course. You'll need to go to the state library in Raleigh. They have them all on microfilm."

"Thanks!" yelled Dru over her shoulder.

Now she needed to catch the school bus! It was frequently late in the morning, but it was never, ever, late leaving school. This end of the hall, the freshman end, was already clear of students. They had learned to grab their books and rush out to the bus in two minutes flat.

She was trotting down the hall toward the steps when she suddenly screeched to a halt. There in the hall, in no apparent hurry, were Brad and Sarah. Sarah was leaning with her back against her locker. Brad was standing very close to her, one hand propped against the locker near her head, and the other holding his book bag which was slung over his shoulder. They were looking silently into each other's eyes, and as Dru watched, Brad bent and softly kissed Sarah's lips.

Dru was on the point of backing up quietly and heading for the steps, when an angry voice rang out.

"Here, you two! None of that in the hall! We can't have that stuff going on here!"

Brad and Sarah jumped. They turned their shocked faces to stare at Mr. Abbott who was standing angrily, his hands on his hips.

"Oh! It's you, Miss Pollock! It seems to me that you would hold off for a while after what happened yesterday!" He glanced at Brad contemptuously. "Is this another one of your boyfriends?"

Sarah and Brad were too dumbfounded to speak. They could only stand, staring helplessly.

"Run on along!" Mr. Abbott sneered. "But, this is a warning. Don't let me catch you out here in the hall again. I've had enough of this kind of stuff out of you!"

Sarah's face was flaming red, but Brad's was pale with anger. Without a word, she turned and took her books from her locker. She shrugged off Brad's hand and walked alone down the steps, her back unnaturally straight.

Brad whirled abruptly and almost bumped into Dru.

"Come on!" she said. She knew that now was not the time to say another word.

Sarah was already sitting at the front of the bus, her head turned toward the window, and she didn't look at them as they brushed past. Brad and Dru sat silently, unaware of the usual noise. Dru could see that his eyes were fixed on the back of Sarah's head, but she stared out the window all the way home. When they reached the stop at Brannock Hall, she left the bus quickly, and without turning walked off toward her house. Brad watched her go, but he didn't attempt to follow her. When they entered the house, he went straight to his room.

Dru let him go without speaking. She knew he needed time to be alone, but she was not sorry. She had plenty to do, and there was not much time left!

She found Aunt Kate sitting in the parlor at her desk.

"Aunt Kate!" Dru said abruptly. "I need to go to Raleigh tomorrow. How can I arrange it?"

"I need to go, too," Aunt Kate said. "I'll take you."

"Well," thought Dru as she walked away. "That was easy!" That conversation would have lasted about fifteen minutes with Mom, and they would probably have ended up mad at each other. It had taken about fifteen seconds to reach an agreement with Aunt Kate. Despite everything, time was going by too fast. She was going to miss Aunt Kate and Brannock Hall.

For the first time in memory Brad skipped supper, and after one quick glance at Dru, Aunt Kate did not ask questions. They both ate quietly, preoccupied. Afterwards Dru offered to clean up, and was careful to take special pains with the job. In the end, she even mopped the floor before going upstairs.

"Brad," she asked through the hole, "did you call Sarah?"

"Yes," he answered shortly. "She wouldn't talk to me."

Dru spent a restless evening, and she knew Brad did, too, though they didn't speak again.

# NEWSPAPERS

The alarm rang at 5:00, and Dru shot out of bed, alert and wide awake. She tried to be quiet as she shampooed her hair and blew it dry. Maybe she should wear something besides jeans today. She pulled on a white mini skirt and a sleeveless apricot sweater.

Make-up, too, she thought. She carefully applied blush and eye liner. She stood at the mirror and surveyed the result. Not bad! Her blond hair gleamed, the apricot lipstick matched the sweater, and her tennis legs, lean and tan, looked great under the white skirt.

She and Aunt Kate rode in companionable silence to Raleigh. They made arrangements to meet at 4:30 that afternoon, and Dru waved good-bye as she ran up the marble steps of the library. There was a counter to the right just inside the door, and one of the woman working behind it directed her to the basement where the microfilm was kept.

Dru shortly found herself seated in front of a machine with a large screen and several knobs. She had a box full of rolled films on which were transferred the Brannock County Free Press editions from 1855-1860. She inserted the first one and turned the forward knob. Sheets of print zoomed past on the screen in front of her eyes  She settled down and for the next two hours carefully skimmed through the files.

At first she was almost amused by the old newspapers. The editor made no attempt to report the news objectively. His articles fairly bristled with opinions. He was angry at everybody: politicians were knaves and scoundrels, businessmen were poltroons, preachers were sinners and transgressors, railroad managers were rascals. Other newspaper editors were the worst of all: villains, vipers, devils! In these years before the Civil War, tempers were high and almost no one agreed with anyone else on any subject. Even the slightest disagreements seemed blown out of proportion.

Dru shook her head in wonder. It was sad. Perhaps if the newspaper men had been calmer, they wouldn't have stirred up so much trouble. All of this anger must have contributed to the war. It was dangerous!

Brannock Hall was mentioned a few times, but she was surprised to find other great plantations mentioned more frequently. It was hard for her to remember that it was only one of several great homes that had dotted the countryside. Strange that Brannock Hall, alone, had survived.

Dru ran across several announcements for slave auctions, and there were frequent notices of rewards offered for runaways. She stopped and rubbed her tired eyes. Her mind began to drift back in time. She could almost feel the heat of a summer day on her skin. There was an open air market, perhaps located on this very spot. People were chained to posts in the corners. Some of them sat crying together in groups, clutching each other for comfort. Others sat dumbly swatting at the flies around their lips and eyes. Among them walked white men, wearing boots and wide hats. An auction master issued orders in a sharp voice. At one end of the market was a square wooden block on which a woman stood quietly, her head bowed. Several laughing men stood around her. One of them reached out and poked her with his riding crop.

Dru jerked awake. It wasn't possible that Adalicia would have run away and left Emily and Daniel at the mercy of LeFevre! He would have sold them at a market just like that. She was about to insert another film when her eye was caught by a familiar name. There under one of the notices about a runaway slave was mention of Quaker Ben. Although nothing could actually be proven, there was the suspicion that he might be involved in the slave's disappearance. The article suggested that Quaker Ben present himself to clear his name of these "scurrilous charges." There was a $500 reward offered for the slave's return: a lot of money in those days.

Dru sighed. She wished it was Quaker Ben that Adalicia was meeting in the woods. He would have been the perfect person to help her arrange Emily and Daniel's escape. But Dru knew that wasn't possible. Adalicia told her father she was eloping with a man she loved. Obviously, that wasn't old Quaker Ben.

She stretched and rubbed her eyes. She had to force herself to concentrate as she inserted another film in the machine. Almost immediately, she found what she wanted.

There, on the first page of the paper, dated May 5, 1860, was the announcement of Adalicia's murder!

*BEAUTIFUL MISTRESS OF BRANNOCK*
*HALL FOUND MURDERED*
*MYSTERIOUS LOVER*
*SOUGHT IN HER DEATH*

*Mistress Adalicia Brannock, six-teen-year-old daughter of Robert Jus-tin Brannock, owner of Brannock Hall, was found stabbed to death last night. Her distraught aunt, Miss Sa-rah Brannock, informs this paper that Mistress Brannock was murdered dur-ing an unauthorized elopement. Her father has been notified, and is pres-ently making his way home.*

*The reputation of a young woman is as beautiful as it is fragile, and that of a Southern woman especially so! It is painful to report that according to accounts widely circulated in the county, Mistress Brannock had grown wild and unrestrained during her father's absence. She is said to have formed an alliance with a mysteri-ous young man which was not ap-*

*proved by those in authority, and which was conducted in the utmost secrecy. It is believed by her aunt that he was an unprincipled villain who wooed her for her wealth. The priceless Brannock pearls, which were given to Mistress Brannock by her father on the occasion of her sixteenth birthday, have been discovered missing, and are thought to be the motive for her murder.*

*The circumstances surrounding her death must be an unbearable burden to her father. We can only advise him to remove all thoughts of his unworthy daughter from his heart and grieve for her no longer. Let him instead be thankful that she died before she could travel further down this path of sin!*

*During the disturbance created by the discovery of Mistress Brannock's body, two slaves escaped. A reward of $500 each is offered for their return.*

There followed a description of Daniel and Emily. No reward was offered for the discovery of Adalicia's murderer.

Dru was horrified! She sat motionless, staring at the paper. She kept swallowing the gorge that was rising in her throat. Murdered! Beautiful Adalicia! At last she got up and staggered to the bathroom where she splashed cold water on her face. She leaned her forehead against the cool tile of the bathroom wall until she felt her stomach muscles begin to relax.

After a few minutes, she returned to the machine and forced herself to wind through the remainder of the tapes, but she could find nothing else. The murder of Adalicia was quickly forgotten. Brannock Hall and its inhabitants were not as important as the great war which threatened the country.

Dru was waiting outside for Aunt Kate when she arrived in the late afternoon. She didn't know how long she had been sitting on the low stone wall. She felt someone very close to her had died a horrible death, and that the lies spread by Aunt Sarah and repeated in the paper had been handed down from generation to generation. No one had tried, in all that time, to discover the truth. Adalicia was remembered as a thief and a liar and a disgrace to the family name.

## BRAD'S SATURDAY

Brad spent a restless night. He tossed around for hours after finally turning out his light, but slept late that morning knowing it was Saturday. When he awoke at mid-morning, his first thoughts were of Sarah. He had to repress the impulse to jump out of bed and phone her. He went to bed feeling disturbed and depressed, but he awoke angry! Sarah had no right to be mad at him. True, he had kissed her, and that had been the cause of the trouble with Mr. Abbott, but it wasn't as if he made a habit of kissing girls at school. And, there was something else, he thought with a pang. She kissed him back!

The long day stretched ahead of him. He began to wish he had gone to Raleigh with Dru. He wandered over to the phone and almost picked it up, but calling Sarah was out.

Definitely out! There was no tennis practice until 4:00, there were no more letters in the attic. There was nothing to do except work in the old kitchen, he thought listlessly. He could at least clean a few more pieces before Aunt Kate came home, though he'd have to wait for her to price them.

The warm spring sunshine greeted him as he opened the back door, and immediately he felt more cheerful. As he walked toward the kitchen, the mossy old bricks under his bare feet were damp and a little slimy. He wiggled his toes. It felt good.

Just inside the kitchen gate there was a wooden bench, painted white to match the picket fence. A dogwood tree, bursting with pink blossoms, shaded it. He sat down and looked around him. He liked this little kitchen garden. The old cooks had planted it with sage, rosemary, thyme, and mint. Aunt Kate kept it neatly mowed, and a bright row of tulips nodded gaily along the fence. He stretched lazily, enjoying the sunshine as he rose to his feet.

Pushing open the heavy door, he entered the gloom of the old kitchen and stood quietly looking around. Suddenly he realized he missed Dru and Aunt Kate. He never thought about it before, but this place was spooky. In fact, besides the cemetery, it was the only spooky place at Brannock Hall. They hadn't had time yet to rig electric lights, and the only light that entered the room were the weak rays which filtered through the filthy windows. There was a small, clean space near the center of the kitchen where they had been working, but cobwebs still festooned the corners and back areas, and dust covered everything. Strange lumps and weird shapes seemed to bulge out of the gloom. He felt his skin begin to crawl, and he glanced nervously toward the door. Maybe he should prop it open. Let in some light and warm air.

He turned around and pushed the door. It wouldn't open! He pushed again, harder. It was stuck tight. In growing panic, he repeatedly banged it with his shoulder, running against it with all his strength. A clammy sweat began to break out on his forehead and his heart was leaping beneath his thin shirt. It was happening again! The room was growing cold, and he began to shiver. He felt dizzy from panic and the nauseating smell. Reaching out blindly, his hand touched a heavy wooden stool. Lifting it over his head, he ran panting toward the windows, ready to break the glass.

Suddenly, he felt his arms almost wrenched out of their sockets as the stool was jerked from his hands and sent crashing into the back. There was a violence in the air like static electricity, and the hairs on his arms and legs were tingling. He could actually hear the hairs on his head snapping. Objects began to fly around the room and crash into things. He ducked as a shovel whizzed dangerously past his left ear. He protected his head with his arms, and began backing up. Something struck his right elbow with a heavy thud and left his arm hanging, numbed. Ignoring the pain in his useless arm, he kept moving backward in a blind panic. His last conscious thought was that he was in trouble and there was no one else at home. He was at the mercy of the ghost!

His next conscious thought was groggy. Someone was shaking him. His head ached terribly, and his arms and legs were so heavy, he couldn't move them. He faintly heard a voice crying out from a long distance, but he couldn't make out what it was saying. Somebody was pouring something cold on his forehead. It felt good! Gradually his eyes began to focus, and he painfully turned his head. Bending over him, blue eyes wide with concern, was Adalicia. She was wearing her thick, dark hair pulled back in a loose knot, just as it had been in her portrait.

Brad was confused. He propped himself up on one elbow and stared groggily at her.

"Don't try to move yet!" she spoke. She pushed him back down to the floor.

Brad relaxed backward. It was Sarah.

"You're hurt! I'm going to call an ambulance; but you need to lie quietly while I'm gone. It won't take but a minute."

Brad stretched out a weak hand to detain her, but he was still too dizzy to speak. She was gone before he could react. He lay back and tried to focus on what had happened.

Suddenly, in a sickening wave, he remembered. The ghost! It had attacked him. He tried to struggle up, but fell back down with a cry of pain. Sarah! She mustn't be alone! He managed to prop himself on one elbow facing the door, but she was back almost immediately. She had a blanket with her which she spread over him. He tried to speak, but she gently covered his mouth with her hand, and his body began to relax beneath the warmth of the blanket. Weakly he looked around.

The sun was streaming in through the open door, and the mysterious lumps and eerie shapes had turned back into churns and stools and old pieces of furniture. It was impossible to tell what happened in here, he thought. The place was such a messy jumble, and almost everything in it was already broken. A few more things smashed against the walls didn't matter.

"Look!" exclaimed Sarah suddenly. "This must be what hit you when you fall off the loft." She was kneeling beside him, holding something in her hands.

Brad almost gasped aloud. Sarah was holding an iron chandelier. It's base was a slender circle with six candle holders attached at regular intervals along its top edge. It had been suspended from the ceiling by a thin chain which was still attached to it. Brad's head was beginning to ache, and he was fading in and out of consciousness. He stared stupidly at the black rosebud which seemed to coil and twist along its side.

Sarah broke through his thoughts. She had been examining the wound on top of his head with careful fingers. "When you fell, you must have grabbed the chandelier; then it broke loose from the ceiling and fell on you somehow. Your head is still bleeding. You'll need stitches."

They could hear the scream of the siren as the ambulance turned into the drive. Almost immediately two men with a stretcher came bustling in, and Brad found himself being hustled on board and carried away before he could object.

"Sarah!" he managed to call. "Thanks!"

She gave him a radiant smile, but all she said was, "We need to talk!"

Sarah was waiting on the porch for Aunt Kate and Dru when they returned home in the late afternoon, and without getting out of the car, they drove straight to the hospital. On the way Sarah told them about going to Brannock Hall about noon and finding the back door standing open. No one answered her, and she was growing a little worried until she remembered the old kitchen. She walked back to it on the chance Brad and Dru were spending the day working in it. She was shocked to find the door propped open and Brad lying in the middle of the floor in a pool of his own blood.

"I think he must have fallen from the loft and was struck on his head by an old chandelier, but he couldn't talk much. I've been worried all afternoon. My parents aren't at home today, and the hospital won't release information to me because I'm not his next of kin." She was close to tears.

Dru was worried sick, and one glance at Aunt Kate's face and hands clenched around the wheel told her that she was worried, too. Aunt Kate screeched into the hospital parking lot on two wheels, ignoring the frown of the attendant. They hurried down the hospital corridor and pushed open Brad's door.

He was propped against a large pile of pillows, sipping a soda through a straw and polishing off a big piece of chocolate cake. A color TV mounted on the wall above his head was tuned to a game show, and a nurse was seated beside the bed laughing with him. His right arm was in a sling and the top of his head was covered with bandages. Both eyes regarded them through huge, purple shiners, but he grinned at them happily.

"Well!" said Aunt Kate in obvious relief. She slumped down on a chair and began to catch her breath.

Sarah and Dru were still clasping each other's hands nervously. "Tomorrow," resolved Dru, "I'll bring him all his favorite things: Snickers and Moon Pies and Astro Pops!"

But she couldn't help wonder as she met the warning look in his eyes how long she would have to wait before she could hear what really happened. Sarah's theory that he fell off the loft and was struck by the chandelier didn't make a lot of sense. It was enough right now that he was alive and not hurt seriously, but the timing was bad. There was so much to do, and so many things they still needed to find out. She could use his help!

# YELLOWED PHOTOGRAPHS

Dru stood in the narrow street and contemplated the scene before her. She could have been standing in another century she thought to herself. Facing her was a small brick building which contained the Historical Society archives. It seemed to rest lazily in the sunshine. On one side of it stood a hardware store whose fly-specked windows looked as if they hadn't been washed in fifty years. Across the street was a small, grassy park where the statue of a Confederate soldier stood on its pedestal, bravely facing north.

As Dru climbed the archive steps, she examined with interest the deep gouges in the old brick which Aunt Kate said had been put there by Yankee cannon shot. It was all kind of nice, she thought. Back home, this little corner would have been torn down and paved over a long time ago.

Inside, at a wooden desk, sat a bored girl. She kept her finger in the book she was studying as she glanced up at Dru.

"Do you have a permit?" she asked.

Dru handed her the permit Aunt Kate had arranged for her and the girl stamped it. "What you want is in the basement," she said indifferently, opening her book.

Dru carefully stepped down the narrow flight of stairs. The small, cramped basement was cluttered, but clean. Someone had painted the walls a brilliant white. Filing cabinets and boxes were everywhere, but after a few minutes, she could see there was order to the system.

Along one wall, the filing cabinets were packed with newspapers and pamphlets arranged in chronological order. A quick look through the year marked 1860 told her that most of the newspapers were ones she had already read on the microfilm. She decided to skip those, and look through the years marked 1861-1865 to see if there was any mention of Brannock Hall which would give her a clue about Adalicia's murderer.

The papers from those years depressed her. They contained almost nothing but war news.

So much killing! The lists of the war dead on both sides covered rows of newsprint, and some of the dead soldiers were no older than Brad. She had to force herself to scan the papers without thinking too much about Brad lying dead on a battlefield! She couldn't waste time.

After an hour, she had found nothing except the mention of Robert's death in a skirmish near Kinston in 1862, and she knew the task was too big for her. She needed to come back with Brad and probably Sarah, too. The papers were so full of war news that the local news was hidden away on the inside pages. She looked at the remaining drawers stuffed with papers, and sighed. They needed to make a careful search: scanning missed too much.

She closed the drawer and stood dejectedly, before she could bring herself to climb the steps and check out with the bored girl. She began to walk idly around the room, examining the labels on the boxes. In a corner under the steps she found a box marked "photographs." Brad would be interested in that. The box was filled with hundreds of old black and white photographs taken during the Civil War. They were yellow with age, and some of them were blotched with water stains, but Dru exclaimed aloud in amazement! She had known there were cameras in the nineteenth century because she had seen pictures of stiff people with their hair parted in the middle, but she had no idea photographs like these existed.

There were pictures of soldiers lounging in front of their tents. There were pictures of officers on horseback, their hollow eyes fixed sadly on the distance. There were terrible pictures of bloated corpses strewn about in trenches, and pictures of hundreds of bodies left lying in the mud after a battle. Could one of them be "dearest Papa?" One showed a riderless horse tied next to a framed picture of his dead master; a Union flag was draped around the frame. Some of them were of women and children. There was a black woman and a white woman dressed almost alike, with their hands around each other's waists. They were standing in front of the ruins of a burned house. Dru was fascinated. These were amazing photographs, and she couldn't wait to show Brad.

Suddenly she froze. "Wow!" she exclaimed.

She unconsciously dropped the other photographs and slowly rose to her feet, staring at the one she held in her hands.

"Wow!" she exclaimed, again.

Gazing back at her was the most handsome man she had ever seen! He was standing in front of a wagon, and one booted foot was propped on its frame. He was dressed in black pants and a white shirt with loose sleeves, and in his hands he held a black, wide-brimmed hat. The sun falling on his left shoulder caught his hair, making it glow like a flame around his face, and she noticed that his shoulders were broad and unusually strong as though he was used to hard work. He could have been a movie star wearing a nineteenth century costume, but there was something special about him. He seemed to be watching her with as much interest as she was watching him, and she had the feeling he was making an honest judgment. She wondered who he was.

Her attention was caught by the wagon. There were strange tools attached to its side. She could make out a pair of long, heavy tongs, and surely that was a bellows. Dru froze! She could feel her blood run cold, and the tiny hairs on the back of her neck began to prickle. Slowly, almost fearfully, she turned the picture over. On the back, in faded brown ink, were written two words, "Quaker Ben."

Time seemed to stand still and she stood in a daze, her eyes were fixed sightlessly on the faint writing, but her mind was whirling. When she finally emerged from her daze, she realized she held in her hands an important piece of the puzzle. She knew now what had happened to Adalicia. She didn't have positive proof, but she knew.

Furtively, she glanced up the steps, and seeing the girl behind the desk still reading her book, she tucked the picture under her shirt. Brad had to see this! She ran up the stairs and guiltily approached the desk.

The bored girl scarcely glanced up. "Here's your permit," she said. "You'll have to sign out on that register."

Irrationally, Dru was annoyed. The girl didn't care what happened. Anybody could walk out with anything! They might as well hire a goldfish to guard the archives. But, she thought as she ran down the front steps, she was glad she had the picture. She would return it the next day. Right now she had to talk to Brad.

She found him looking much better. She had visited him that morning, but he was too weak for her to stay long. She had told him briefly about her search through the micro-film and Adalicia's murder, but she wasn't sure how much he remembered. He looked more alert now, and his brown eyes smiled at her cheerfully through their blackened sockets. He was ordering things from a dinner menu a nurse had given him earlier. Dru could see a lot of black checks.

"Just wait 'till I show you!" she exclaimed, hurriedly pulling up a chair. She withdrew the picture from her shirt and thrust it into his hand. His reaction was not quite what she expected.

He glanced at it. "Good looking guy, in a way," he said. "Who is he? The latest sitcom talent?"

"He's not an actor, stupid! Look again!"

This time Brad gave it a closer scrutiny, and as he looked, his interest grew.

"Well?" said Dru.

Brad looked at her curiously. "Well, what?" he asked.

"Turn it over!" she demanded.

Brad turned it over and looked at the name on the back. Suddenly it hit him! His body jerked off the pillow.

"Ouch!" he cried, and lay back down. "This is Quaker Ben! But ... ." his voice trailed off.

He stared at Dru.

"Yes!" Dru answered. "We thought he was an old man. We never thought he might be young and handsome."

She looked expectantly at Brad while he studied the picture. She could see his mind begin to work just as hers had done.

"This changes everything," he said at last. "Do you think it's possible Quaker Ben was the man she loved? Was he the one she was meeting in the woods?"

"Of course he was! They were made for each other! She probably contacted him secretly because she had heard of him and wanted him to save Daniel and Emily, or maybe they met while he was making kitchen tools at Brannock Hall, but however they met, they were bound to fall in love."

"Obviously," grinned Brad wickedly. "It wouldn't have taken weeks of secret meetings in the woods to arrange Daniel's and Emily's escape. They had other things on their minds."

Dru ignored him. "They must have planned their elopement and the escape for the same night. Adalicia threw us off the track when she told her father she wasn't taking anything of his with her. We should have realized she wouldn't have thought of Daniel and

Emily as property."

"Something went terribly wrong," Brad said. "Adalicia was murdered that night. Somebody killed her, and spread vicious rumors about her to cover up."

After a few moments silence, Dru spoke. "Well, we know who it was, though we don't have actual proof. Quaker Ben wasn't a murderer, and nobody else could have done it but LeFevre. The only other person who hated her was Aunt Sarah, and Aunt Sarah wouldn't stoop to actual murder, though she didn't mind murdering her reputation."

"You're right," agreed Brad. "All the lies about Adalicia and the lover who killed her for her pearls were a good cover-up. LeFevre probably planted the idea in Aunt Sarah's head, and she was happy to spread the news!"

Dru sat staring at the picture of Quaker Ben. The idea that he had killed Adalicia was absurd.

She spoke slowly. "I can almost work it out. Adalicia must have arranged an escape date with Ben, and smuggled Daniel and Emily out. Emily would have been easy because no one watched her at night, but not Daniel. She probably had to ask one of the other slaves to steal the key to the shed from LeFevre. She didn't know LeFevre had spies everywhere. He must have known her plans almost immediately."

"Right." Brad thought for a moment. "He might have pushed her into taking action earlier than she planned. Remember how excited he was in his last letter? He called her a 'wench,' and said she played right into his hands. All he had to do was keep his spies out! He knew she would do something to save Emily and Daniel."

Dru's face was angry. "He was a real jerk!" There were tears in her eyes. "I bet he stabbed her in the back. He wouldn't have the courage to stab her from the front. In a way, that was good, though. She probably never knew what happened."

Brad didn't like to think about it. He suppressed thoughts of the beautiful girl running through the woods to meet the three people she loved most in the world. In just a few more minutes they would all escape into freedom! How did they feel when they found her body?

Dru broke into his thoughts. "We still don't know exactly what happened to Ben and Daniel and Emily."

"Well, we do know Emily and Daniel escaped because a reward was offered for their capture. Ben probably delivered them to the underground railroad and never came back. Aunt Kate told us he disappeared suddenly and was never heard of again."

Dru thought this over. "I'm really surprised LeFevre let them escape. He could have stopped them; but the newspapers definitely say two slaves escaped in the confusion."

"They must have escaped. You said there's no mention of their capture in the newspapers, and they're not buried in the cemetery. LeFevre must have let them go on purpose. Maybe he thought they'd talk if he kept them. With them gone and Adalicia dead and Robert off at war, LeFevre had control of the plantation. There was nobody to stop him but Aunt Sarah, and she was no problem."

"Yeah," agreed Dru. "LeFevre would rather lose Daniel and Emily and blame Adalicia's death on a mysterious lover than risk calling attention to himself, because he was the only other obvious suspect. Aunt Sarah was the perfect accomplice; she was delighted to spread the rumors about 'poor' Adalicia and her wickedness. All LeFevre had to do was sit back and look sad!"

"All of them played into his hands," said Brad. "Even Robert. It was too much for him to take. The whole county must have been buzzing about it. Aunt Sarah saw to that. He didn't even make a serious effort to find the lover who supposedly murdered her. He buried her in the slave cemetery, and left."

"He must have still loved her a little bit," said Dru sadly. She remembered the beautiful marble gravestone with its delicate rosebud which lay under the branches of the old yew.

"Yeah, but he was too weak to stand up for her. He went away and was killed in battle. His brother, Webb, was at war too, and didn't have time to take charge. LeFevre knew he could count on four or five years when he could cheat and steal and grow rich off the Brannock property. I wonder what happened to him?"

They sat in silence, but after a few minutes, Brad remembered that he hadn't told Dru what had happened to him in the kitchen the day he was injured. He had just started when he was interrupted by an attendant bearing a tray heaped high with covered dishes. Aunt Kate entered the room close behind him.

"Mercy!" she said mildly as she saw the piles of food under the rounded covers Brad was busily removing.

Brad grinned. "I gotta keep up my strength."

"Let me know if you want more, Bud," the orderly said cheerfully as he opened the door. "There's plenty more where that came from. Nobody else likes it."

"Well," said Aunt Kate as she watched Brad tuck into the food. "I expect you're hungry too, Dru. I'll take you home and we can get something to eat. Maybe I'll come back later, though you don't look as if you need me."

"I don't," said Brad, clicking the TV remote control. "This is the life!"

He waved to them as they left, but as the door closed, he had a moment's worry. He hadn't warned Dru not to go in the old kitchen! But almost immediately, he relaxed. They had discovered the secret. They knew what happened to Adalicia. All the puzzle pieces had fallen into place. Even though they didn't have positive proof, they had a lot of circumstantial evidence. LeFevre's lies were proven by his own diary, and he was the only one who could possibly have murdered Adalicia.

She was not the wild girl people thought she was. She was meeting the man she loved and trying to rescue two helpless people.

People today would have a lot of sympathy for that. She was a real heroine!

The ghost could rest in peace. There was no more danger for any of them.

## TRAP DOOR

The next morning Dru and Aunt Kate found Brad packed and ready to leave the hospital, but when they got home, his head began to ache again and he went straight to bed. He slept through the afternoon, not even awakening for dinner. Dru was disappointed. She had counted on a long talk. She still didn't know what had happened in the old kitchen. To make matters worse, Aunt Kate drove away soon after lunch with a large briefcase.

Dru fretted through the long afternoon. There was nothing to do in the house and Sarah didn't answer her phone. She thought about working in the old kitchen, but she couldn't leave Brad upstairs alone. She felt deserted by everybody: Aunt Kate, Brad, Sarah - even the ghost.

Aunt Kate hurried home to a late supper.

Dru would have been glad for a little conversation, but Aunt Kate seemed preoccupied. Dru wandered upstairs after supper, and after checking on Brad, went to bed early. She drifted off into a troubled sleep.

She slept badly, her dreams haunted by Adalicia. She was running after her through the woods, trying desperately to reach her before LeFevre, but her feet seemed too heavy to lift. Adalicia was running so swiftly she was almost out of sight, and Dru panted with the struggle to keep up. She opened her mouth to scream, but all she could manage were stifled grunts.

Suddenly Adalicia's screams broke through her nightmare, piercing the night again and again! She jerked awake to find Adalicia's screams merging with the sound of sirens as they shrieked past the house.

She lay listening, trying to calm her breathing. There seemed to be several vehicles with wailing sirens, but she was too confused to count clearly. Squinting in the dark, she could just make out the hands of her watch: two-ten. She lay down again and tried to go back to sleep, but her heart was still pounding. She was thankful Brad was in the next room!

She spoke softly. "Brad!"

He answered immediately. "Yeah?"

"Are you awake?" She knew it was a stupid question, but she wanted to hear his voice.

"Yeah," he answered. "Did the sirens wake you?"

"Yes!"

"I wonder what happened? I haven't heard a siren this late since we've lived here."

They lay quietly in the dark, both wide awake.

"Are you hungry?" Dru asked. She remembered he had slept through supper.

"Yeah," Brad answered. "I'm starved!"

"I'll get a snack," she offered.

She padded out the door in her bare feet and down the back steps into the kitchen. Her hand was groping for the light switch when she stopped in surprise. There was a pale glimmer of light outside the window. Moving to the back door, she looked out into the night. Visible above the thick boxwood hedge was a dim, greenish glimmer coming from the old kitchen. She stood watching it for a few minutes.

"That's funny!" she thought.

The pale glow didn't flicker like a fire or a candle, and it didn't move around like a person with a flashlight. It acted like a stationary electric light, but there was no electricity in the old kitchen. She watched in silence for a few minutes. She couldn't be sure, but it seemed to be growing bigger; almost as if it were creeping down the walk toward the house!

Turning swiftly, she ran up the steps and knocked on Aunt Kate's door. There was no answer. Quietly, she pushed it open and peered inside. The room was empty. Aunt Kate's bed covers were thrown back, and the closet door was standing open as though she had been in a hurry.

"Brad!" she said, entering his room. "There's the strangest light coming from the old kitchen, and Aunt Kate is gone."

Brad struggled stiffly out of bed, but Dru could see he had regained much of his strength. The long sleep had been good for him. She followed him down the steps and stood beside him. They looked out the back door. The light was still glowing with it's strange phosphorescence.

Brad regarded it silently for a long time. He seemed to be struggling with himself. At last he spoke. "I think I'd better check it out," he said quietly. His face was a pasty white and the dark circles around his bruised eyes looked like a mask. Dru could tell he was frightened.

She followed him into his room and to her surprise, he began to rummage around in the bottom of his wardrobe. He spoke to her over his shoulder as he pulled out stacks of the heavy ski clothing they had no use for here.

"Go put on all your heavy stuff: sweaters, thermal underwear, ski jacket. Things like that. It doesn't matter how hot you get. The padding will give you protection in case the ghost gets violent."

He was panting with the effort of pulling a heavy, woolen turtle-neck over his bandaged head.

Dru ran to her room and dressed as quickly as possible in layers of thermal underwear and thick pants. She grabbed her down-filled vest and ran back to Brad's room. He was pulling on a ski cap with his good left hand.

A few minutes later they silently pushed open the back door and stood together on the porch. The night was dark and only a few faint stars managed to prick through the muggy atmosphere. Above their heads, a pale gibbous moon hung like a polished half dime in the sky. Somewhere a screech owl uttered its unearthly whinny. Despite the heat she was already feeling, Dru shivered. She took a deep breath and touched Brad's arm.

"Here!" he hissed. He handed her a hefty flashlight. "I tied a cord to the handle so you can hang it around your neck. Don't turn it on unless you have to. We don't want to frighten it away."

The solid weight of the flashlight reassured Dru, and she followed Brad down the steps. As they stepped quietly onto the brick walkway, the glow from the old kitchen suddenly flared brightly and burned out! Dru gasped and reached out to put her hand on Brad's shoulder. Stumbling blindly in the dark, they groped their way over the uneven bricks. When they reached the gate, they stopped to let their eyes adjust. The kitchen loomed in front of them: pitch black, and quiet as death.

There was no doubt in either of their minds that they were in touch with a dangerous force which was waiting for them behind the old door, but it never occurred to them to turn back. The heavy clothing they were wearing suddenly seemed pitiful protection against whatever power might be unleashed on them. The very air around them seemed to pulsate and groan. The familiar chill was beginning to creep inward toward their skins, and the nauseating odor seemed to ooze from the cracks around the door. Dru gagged and Brad steadied her with his good hand.

"Come on!" he said.

He pushed open the gate and, moving at a crouch approached the door. He was putting out a tentative hand to touch it, when it burst open with an impatient bang. A great vortex of musty air sucked them inside and threw them to the floor. Behind them, the heavy door slammed shut.

Dru lay stunned. She could hear objects whizzing past her in the pitch blackness, and tried to protect her head with her arms. She could feel Brad's body pressed next to hers and, remembering his injuries, she flung her left arm around him. An angry, whining noise began to fill the room. It rose and fell in intensity. Dru pressed her head against Brad's shoulder trying to shut it out. It was almost more than she could bear!

But as she crouched there on the floor, something began to happen to her. She felt herself growing angry! This door slamming and throwing things was a simple temper tantrum. She remembered Brett Ashley Moore. He was a spoiled three-year-old brat she used to baby-sit, and he acted exactly like this.

Dru suddenly exploded. "Quiet!" she yelled.

Abruptly, the noise stopped! There was a surprised pause. Brad uncovered his ears, and waited in stupefied silence.

"We need light!" Dru demanded.

After a split second's hesitation, the room was suffused with the same dull green glow they had seen from the house.

Brad stared at Dru in amazement.

Dru stood up. "That's better!" she yelled. "Now, show us what you want!"

Immediately, there was movement in the shadows above their heads. The rosebud chandelier began to whip back and forth.

"Watch out! Duck!" Brad screamed as it broke loose and came crashing down, narrowly missing them.

"That was close!" Brad breathed. "We could'uv been killed!"

"Who put it back up there?" Dru hissed.

"I don't know," Brad whispered in mild disgust. "I missed out on what happened in here while I was vacationing in the hospital."

Dru turned around, gazing blindly into the shadows. "Okay!" she shouted. "Okay! We see the chandelier! What else?"

The room seemed to hum and vibrate like an electric magnet. Suddenly there was a burst of wild confusion in the corner under the loft. An oak cupboard crashed to the floor, and heavy wooden objects were slung wildly about, crashing into the shadows and splintering against each other. Brad blanched. He knew they were in terrible danger. If they were struck by one of the hurled objects, the thick padding they were wearing would be of little help.

Then, suddenly he was angry, too!

"Hey!" he screamed in alarm. "Go easy on those antiques! They're worth a lot of money!"

There was a surprised pause, and then one other object was thrown angrily into a corner.

"Yep!" thought Dru. "Just like Brett Ashley!"

All was silent except for a slight, impatient humming.

"Maybe it wants us over there," Dru whispered.

They cautiously stepped toward the loft. The vibration changed to a lower pitch.

"Okay!" Brad hissed.

He moved closer to the spot where the cupboard had stood. Dru flicked on her flashlight and flashed it around. The humming was coming in short, energetic bursts like the buzzing of a huge, excited bumble bee.

Dru flicked her light to the brick floor, and suddenly she exclaimed. Faintly visible under the layers of dust was a thick-planked, wooden trap door. An iron ring about six inches in diameter was attached to one end.

"Let's see if it opens!" exclaimed Brad excitedly. He grasped the ring with his good hand and strained, but it was impossible for him to lift. Dru grasped it, too, and they both heaved on it. It rose slightly, but it was too heavy, and they had to let it fall back. Immediately, there was a loud, angry buzzing!

Brad giggled with hysteria. "It sounds like we've disturbed a hive of killer bees!"

"Hush!" hissed Dru. "What are we going to do?"

"Why don't you give us a hand, here!" Brad suddenly yelled angrily. "Where are you when we need you?"

The impatient buzzing grew louder.

"Wait!" said Dru. She grabbed a stool from the shadows and set it near the ring.

"I'll pull it open as far as I can, and you prop it with the stool."

Using all her strength, Dru managed to lift the door about a foot. Brad propped it with the stool and for the next few minutes they strained at the door, gaining inch by inch as they worked to open it. At last, Dru stood with the door balanced upright, her hand still grasping the iron ring. It hesitated momentarily at its peak, then fell to the other side with a powerful clang.

Clouds of dust rose around them and made them cough. They were breathing hard and were wet with the perspiration which ran down their faces and soaked their clothing. Their insulated thermal underwear clung to their bodies in a steaming mass. Brad impatiently pulled the woolen hat from his head and ran his fingers through his sticky hair.

"Where's the air conditioning when we need it?" he demanded loudly.

He was answered by silence. Then the buzzing abruptly started again, became a low, thin wail and died away altogether. They could feel a release of tension as though the power had drained from the room. For a single instant, they were filled with a terrible and unbearable sorrow; then that, too, passed. Dru felt something soft brush her face as the green light slowly dimmed and faded away.

They stood alone in the silence, the beams from their flashlights cutting through the blackness. The quiet old kitchen looked as if it had not been disturbed for generations. The super-charged atmosphere of only a few moments before was replaced by the calm of a peaceful old home.

Dru felt strangely deflated. "It's gone," she said. "I don't think it's coming back." She spoke slowly, almost regretfully.

"Right!" said Brad in relief.

They began to peel off their heavy clothing, dropping it around them on the floor; and soon stood in their pajamas, letting the cool night air play against their hot skins.

Brad spoke first. "It wants us to go down there."

He flashed his light toward the gaping hole. Together, they crouched on the floor and peered into it. By the shine from their flashlights, they could see a stone cellar about fifteen feet square. Like the kitchen, it was draped with cobwebs, and layers of dust covered everything. It looked empty except for several rounded mounds lying on the floor.

"It must have been a storage cellar," Brad said. "It was a cool place to store extra potatoes and vegetables and things like that."

"How'd they get down?" Dru wondered.

They crouched for a moment in confusion

until Brad remembered a wooden ladder that was stored against the wall under the loft. Together they carried it to the cellar and gingerly lowered it.

"Be careful!" Brad grunted. "We don't want it to fall on anything."

"Hey!" Dru exclaimed, as the heavy ladder thunked against the earthen floor. "It fits!"

"Yeah," agreed Brad. "It must have been made for the cellar. You couldn't get in or out without it."

"Well!" Dru turned to Brad and took a deep breath. "Here goes!"

Slinging the flashlight by its cord around her neck, she carefully backed down the ladder into the black hole. Brad was close behind her.

"Yuck!" she said as she stepped onto the floor.

Her bare feet were almost covered by the soft, fuzzy dust. She clenched her toes together. She didn't like to think what might be crawling around inside that dust!

"Yuck!" echoed Brad as his feet stepped off the ladder.

"Don't think about it," advised Dru.

Their flashlights easily penetrated the cobwebs to the corners. The room was small. It's stone walls glistened with a damp seepage which trickled down from between the cracks and was sucked into the dirt floor beneath.

Dru turned and met Brad's eyes, and read in them the same dread she was feeling. Slowly, almost fearfully, they turned and faced the dust covered mounds lying on the floor. There was nothing else in the room. Brad played his light over the nearest one.

"It's only a bag!" exclaimed Dru in relief. She stooped down to touch it, and recoiled in horror! Her involuntary scream bounced off the walls and flung itself out the trap door! She leaped up and threw her arms around Brad, fighting for control. Already, she was ashamed.

Brad patted her back apprehensively. "What is it?" he asked.

Dru's voice was muffled against Brad's shoulder. "It's okay," she gasped. "It's only a skeleton."

Brushing her aside, Brad quickly knelt to see for himself.

"They're all skeletons!" he exclaimed. "There're three of them!"

Dru forced herself to kneel beside him and examine the three bodies in front of them. What had once been living flesh and blood had melted away leaving only a pitiful heap of bones which had gradually been covered by years of sifting dust. Swallowing the gorge rising in her throat, she reached out to touch the filthy rags which covered the nearest one.

"I wish I had a stick," she gagged.

"Here," Brad said, pushing her aside. He used the end of his flashlight to brush away some of the cobwebs.

"Look," he said. "They're holding each other!"

The bones had loosed their grip on muscle and tendon, and had slowly sunk to the ground, but like a throw of pick-up-sticks, they could see a pattern.

After a moment, Dru spoke softly. "The one in the middle has her arms around the one nearest us. The third one has his arms around the other two."

Brad looked at her curiously. "Why did you say 'her,'" he asked.

"Because it's Emily," said Dru softly. "And the other two are Daniel and Quaker Ben."

Brad stretched out his hand and gently touched the skull nearest him. There was nothing to be afraid of here. They knelt reverently beside the bodies for a few minutes, each lost in thought.

Brad began to speak thoughtfully. "You know," he said, "LeFevre didn't murder them and throw their bodies down here."

"He didn't?" Dru looked up in surprise. "Who did, then?"

"Oh, LeFevre put them here, all right, but they weren't dead when he did it. Dead people don't put their arms around each other. He threw them down here alive and pulled the ladder up. They must have been down here for days before they starved to death. There was no way they could get out. Even if they managed to stand on each other's shoulders and push against the trap door, it was too heavy for them."

Dru was too horrified to speak. She thought about them locked down here, screaming for help.

"Nobody came for more than a century," Brad exclaimed, "and now it's too late!"

Involuntarily, Dru reached out a hand as though to help; and it brushed against the ragged clothing which still clung to the nearest body. It crumbled away at her touch and her light caught the gleam of something partially concealed beneath the rags. With a cry she drew out a long, opalescent string of beads.

"The Brannock pearls! The ones LeFevre

claimed her lover murdered her for!"

Brad carefully took them in his hands and looked at them in wonder. "LeFevre must have known Ben had them," he said, "but if they'd ever come to light, they would've blown his cover story about the motive for Adalicia's murder. He probably left them down here on purpose. They weren't going anywhere. He could get them whenever he wanted them."

There was a long silence as they thought about it. "I wonder why he didn't?" Dru asked.

"I don't know. Something happened before he got around to it."

"I suppose we'll have to tell Aunt Kate." Dru sighed and looked at the bodies nestled in the soft dust. "Though it seems a shame to disturb them after all these years. At least we know what happened to them."

"We've also solved the last mystery," Brad said. "We've got our ghost!"

For a second Dru was stunned, then realization dawned. "You mean one of them was the ghost! But...!"

"It has to be," Brad interrupted, rubbing his aching eyes. "Nothing else fits. And, besides, the last thing the ghost did was lead us to the bodies."

"But, which one!"

"I don't know," admitted Brad wearily.

"Well, it certainly wasn't Emily!" Dru exclaimed firmly. "This body must be Ben's," Brad said thoughtfully. "The one in the middle is Emily's. The one on the other side must be Daniel's. His arm is thrown over the other two. That means he died last."

"You're right," Dru agreed.

Suddenly Brad was struck by a thought. He jumped to his feet, and heedless of the clouds of dust raised by his movement, began to explore the stone walls with his light. Dru knelt beside the bodies, watching him.

After a few minutes, he exclaimed, "Here it is!"

Puzzled, Dru joined him. He was closely examining a stone near the base of one wall.

"Shine your light on it, too, Dru! I can hardly read it!"

As she stooped, Dru could see something scratched on the stone. She bent down with Brad to read it.

> *Love burns and flickers.*
> *Wealth ever lies.*
> *Time burns the embers, but*
> *Hate never dies!*
> *Daniel*

Dru stared at it uncomprehendingly.

"Don't you see?" asked Brad. "It's Daniel's curse on LeFevre! Daniel is the ghost! For a while I thought it must be Ben because he was in love with Adalicia, but Daniel loved her too, and he loved her longer. He also had more reason to hate LeFevre. He knew LeFevre murdered Adalicia, and he had to watch Emily slowly die of starvation. Emily's arms are around Ben, so Ben died first."

"Yes!" Dru was excited. "He may even have been injured during the escape and was so weak he didn't live long. Emily was frail, she probably didn't live much longer, but Daniel was a strong man. There's no telling how much longer he lived than the other two! He may have been left alone with their bodies for days."

"He had time to build up a hatred that lasted beyond his actual death," said Brad. "I knew he must have left a message. He had plenty of time. It was the only thing he had to do."

"I hope he can rest now," said Dru, softly touching the stone. "He's done the last thing he can ever do for Adalicia. He's cleared her name for all time."

Brad tenderly felt his bandaged head. "I

don't know why he wanted to hurt me, though. I was trying to help him!"

"I don't think he was deliberately trying to hurt you," Dru answered. "He was just frustrated and didn't know how to control his power. He was dangerous without meaning to be."

Brad crouched silently. He stared at the words which had been so painstakingly scratched on the hard stone. It was still hard to believe the ghost he had been afraid of was Daniel. He smiled ruefully. He was glad he was gone. Daniel would have been a lot more likable in his natural state.

Over their heads, they became aware of hurried footsteps.

"Dru! Brad!" Aunt Kate was calling urgently. "Answer me!"

"Down here, Aunt Kate!" called Dru.

Aunt Kate's head appeared over the rim of the trap door, closely followed by Deputy Randy Travers', and as they watched in amazement, a third head appeared – Ida Lou Duncan's!

## RANDY'S THEORY

Back in the kitchen, Brad and Dru stood at the sink wiping the worst of the dirt off their faces with wet paper towels, and combing at the cobwebs in their hair with their fingers. Aunt Kate heated water for hot tea and sliced a fresh loaf of pound cake. Ida Lou was fussily wiping a damp mop over the dirty footprints on Aunt Kate's otherwise spotless floor.

Randy Travers sat at the table, surveying them all. "Well!" he drawled at last. "A hundred and thirty year old triple murder! I don't suppose y'all got any idea who the perpetrator could'uv been?"

"Yes, we do!" Dru and Brad spoke in unison, and turned eagerly to the table. Between gulps of tea and bits of cake, they took turns telling their story, beginning with what they learned from the attic letters, and ending with what happened that night after they had been wakened by the sirens; but they were careful to leave out all mention of the ghost.

They talked for almost an hour, interrupted only by an occasional "I declare!" or "I had no idea!" from Aunt Kate, and "I really do declare!" from Ida Lou.

"And look, Aunt Kate!" exclaimed Dru at last, drawing something from the pocket of her robe. "Here are Adalicia's pearls!"

This final excitement was too much for Aunt Kate and Ida Lou. They simply threw up their hands in silent amazement.

Randy Travers sat quietly through the story. At the end, he stood up and stretched. "Come on, son," he said. "Let's go on out and examine the scene of the crime before I call the sheriff. Guess I'll have to call the county coroner, too. Regulations. Though I don't think he'll be able to determine the exact time of death on this one, do you?" He clapped Brad on the shoulder as they shut the back door behind them.

Dru looked after them in disgust, and then quickly rose and followed them. This was no time for macho male bonding. Whatever it was they were going to discuss involved her, too.

They walked down the brick walk toward

the old kitchen. Pale fingers of pink were beginning to streak the early dawn sky. Brad was exhausted and his bandaged head and arm were throbbing, but Dru felt exhilarated.

Randy Travers cleared his throat and spoke. "Now, tell me, y'all. What really happened? Have you been having a little trouble with the ghost?"

Brad and Dru stopped dead in their tracks and stared at each other in astonishment.

Dru spoke a little stiffly, "What makes you think anything happened except what we already told you. And exactly what ghost are you referring to?"

"Why the ghost that lives in Brannock Hall, of course. I was a friend of your father's. Didn't Miss Kate tell you that? Him and your Uncle Paul used to spend their summers here, and when I was about thirteen I hung out with 'em. We'd spend the nights in those two bedrooms at the end of the hall, and I tell you, some might funny noises used to come through that hole in the wall. At first we thought it was each other, but we finally figured it out. Got so we couldn't sleep nights, and we'd take our blankets and bed down on the veranda. I was a little younger than your father, and a lot more scared! At last, I quit coming around."

"Dad never told us that!" exclaimed Brad.

"Well, it's not the kind of thing you can talk about. As time went on, he probably forgot about it, or thought it was his imagination, or something. I did. I began to think it was something a bunch of crazy kids dreamed up one summer. It was easy to do, especially since Miss Kate never seemed to sense anything strange."

"We know!" said Dru. They walked quietly down the walk, digesting this new information.

As they opened the old kitchen door, Randy sniffed experimentally. "Well, he's not in here now, anyway. I don't get the scent of catfish rotting in the sunshine."

Dru and Brad laughed shortly, but both were suddenly too overcome by the night's events to want to talk. Randy walked over and looked at the rosebud chandelier.

"Yup!" he said. "Soon's I heard you'd been hit in the head by that thing, I knew the ghost was up to his old tricks. We used to come in here sometimes and find it swaying back and forth. Once, he even threw it at us, but he missed. Next time we came out here, it was hanging back up there again just as pretty as you please. We didn't come back anymore, particularly since Miss Kate didn't want us mucking about in here with her precious antiques. I tell you, we were glad to have an excuse! We did finally figure out who the ghost was, though."

"You did?" exclaimed Brad in amazement. Instantly he was alert, all his tiredness gone.

"Yup!" It was that fool overseer, Jacque LeFevre. He was a wicked man in life, and an even wickeder one in death."

"Oh!" Brad exchanged a glance with Dru. "How did you figure that out?"

"Well, we knew the swinging chandelier must be a clue, so we asked Miss Kate if we could look through the papers in the Historical Society archives. We had the same idea as your sister, here." He looked approvingly at Dru. "Only we were looking for something that happened at a later date. We figured whatever it was probably happened right after the Civil War since Brannock Hall was suddenly boarded up about that time.

"Your Uncle Paul figured there must be some connection, and it turned out he was right. We began looking through the files beginning with 1865. There sure were a lot of them! It took the three of us almost a week to get through that one year."

He laughed in remembrance. "Miss Kate sure was pleased. She thought we were studying those files because we loved history. She thought we'd all grow up to be history professors, or something."

"Uncle Paul did," said Dru.

"That's right!" laughed Randy. "Well, we read all the papers published during the last year of the war. Brannock Hall was mentioned a lot. By that time it was headquarters for a group of men who were supposed to be Union officers, but the editor of the Brannock County Free Press charged they were actually a mix of deserters from both sides who were using Brannock Hall as a center for smuggling and other illegal activities. LeFevre was their leader and he was rich as a king. The Yankees turned a blind eye on his operations because he supplied them with whiskey and things they couldn't get anywhere else. Anyhow, when they left, they spared Brannock Hall.

Soon afterwards the editor was mysteriously murdered, and there was no more mention of Brannock Hall for along time; but we kept on reading because we still hadn't found anything that was connected to the chandelier.

We finished all the war years, and at last

in 1866, the year after the war ended, we found it. Robert's younger brother, Lieutenant Colonel Webb Brannock, came home to claim his rightful place as owner of Brannock Hall. He found LeFevre living in his house like a lord, and he was as mad as a cat in a hurricane!

LeFevre was licked before he began. He didn't put up much of a fight, and Webb tied him up and locked him in the kitchen. Then he rode off to find what was left of the county authorities; but everything was so confused and so much had been burned and destroyed, that it took him two days to find help. When he got back. LeFevre was hanging from the chandelier with the chain twisted around his neck.

It was ruled suicide, though nobody really believed it. There was no chair or anything else to stand on, and the doors were still locked from the outside, and there was no sign of breaking and entering. There was something else: LeFevre's body was covered with terrible bruises and sores. People figured Webb had killed him, but Webb swore LeFevre was alive and unharmed when he left him. The truth was, nobody really cared. By that time everybody left in the county hated LeFevre. Nobody trusted him.

Anyhow, we figured we'd found the answer. LeFevre was either murdered or committed suicide, but his kind of evil never dies. His ghost haunted Brannock Hall for more than a century, and if you and your sister here have finally gotten rid of him, I, for one, am mighty glad!" He clapped Brad on the back.

Brad whistled softly. The last piece of the puzzle clicked into place. Daniel's ghost had been thorough. He had waited for six years until he could take his revenge on LeFevre. Had he tortured him for two days before he finally executed him? Maybe he wanted LeFevre to feel some of the terror Adalicia and Emily and Ben had felt.

"Hate never dies!" Daniel's hatred had lasted beyond the grave. Brad shuddered. He felt almost sorry for LeFevre. He remembered the terror he had felt the night the ghost shook his bed. More than once he and Dru had been in danger from an almost uncontrollable force, and Daniel had not hated them!

But, he remembered suddenly, Daniel had also loved beyond the grave. He had spent one hundred and thirty years trying to clear Adalicia's name. Brad smiled faintly. Despite everything, he was glad he and Dru had been the ones who had finally helped him.

Dru was speaking to Randy. "That's an interesting theory," she was saying politely, but if you and Dad thought LeFevre's ghost was haunting Brannock Hall, why didn't you tell Aunt Kate? She and Great-Grandmama might have been in danger?"

Brad waited with interest to hear what he would say.

Randy hesitated. "Well, you know, it was hard to know how much to tell her. We knew she would be insulted at the thought of a ghost in her precious home, and at last we didn't tell her anything. She didn't seem to be in any danger. The ghost never bothered her. In fact, we always felt safe around her."

Brad nodded, satisfied. "I know exactly what you mean," he yawned, "but you've got the ghost figured wrong." He yawned again. "We'll tell you about it tomorrow, but we can't tonight. We're too tired."

Randy cast a quick glance at Brad's pale face. His legs trembled from weakness and it was only by a great effort of will that he was still standing. Dru's eyes were already closing. Without another word, Randy took them by the arms and supported them down the path and into the house.

As they climbed the steps to their bedrooms, Randy spoke kindly, "I'm going to keep watch down here for the rest of the night. Nothing else will happen, I can promise you that!"

Brad turned, and his tired eyes sparkled from the dark bruises surrounding them which were turning a putrid shade of yellowish green. "Don't worry," he said. "He's not coming back. He's gone forever."

Randy Travers looked at him steadily, then flashed him a thumbs-up sign. He headed for the back door, smothering a yawn.

As Brad opened his bedroom door, the last thing he heard was Ida Lou's voice, chirping excitedly, "Who's gone? Who's gone forever? I hope he hasn't taken anything! These antiques are irreplaceable! Just irreplaceable!"

# MODERN ADALICIA

It seemed like only a few minutes later when Brad groaned and turned over. Every bone in his body ached and the sun streaming through the window hurt his puffy eyes. He squinted in pain and feebly raised his hand to block out the worst of the rays.

"Brad!" Dru was calling through the hole. "Come on! The sheriff is here!"

With a thrill of excitement, Brad flung himself out of bed and grabbed his jeans. He was close behind Dru as she ran down to the kitchen. Outside in the yard, they could see a county van and two ambulances. A group of paramedics were loading a covered stretcher into the back of one of the ambulances, and two reporters were running toward them with a camera. As they watched, one of them lifted the blanket and held it while the other snapped a shot of what was beneath.

They stared into each other's shocked faces. Somehow it seemed wrong to drag Ben and Emily and Daniel from the quiet nineteenth century cellar where they had lain together for so long.

Brad forced himself to turn his eyes away from the window and he was surprised to find Randy Travers, Ida Lou Duncan, and a man he didn't know sitting at the table sipping coffee. Sitting beside Aunt Kate was Sarah, whose blue eyes were regarding him sympathetically. The morning immediately improved! He pulled a chair up and sat down beside her. Dru took the chair on her other side.

Aunt Kate looked up from the paper she was holding. She spoke to them kindly. "It's police procedure," she explained. "They have to examine the bodies and file routine reports, but then I've arranged to have the remains released to me. I'm seeking special permission from the county authorities to have them buried right here at Brannock Hall next to Adalicia."

"Yes," spoke Ida Lou, "and if the county gives us trouble with their rules and regulations, the Historical Society will just have to take steps! They won't cause trouble."

Aunt Kate put down her paper and smiled approvingly at her.

"Good," breathed Dru. She knew Adalicia and Ben and Daniel and Emily belonged together. It was what they would have wanted, and it was the last thing they could do for them.

"Now," said Aunt Kate. "This is Mr. William Henderson. He's the president of the county council and we're finishing up some business here. I think we're through with you for now, Sarah. We'll let you know when the arrangements have been made for you and Eduardo to testify."

Brad and Dru stared at Sarah in amazement as she rose from the table. She smiled politely at Mr. Henderson and shook his hand.

"Come on!" said Brad. He led the way up the steps to Dru's room.

"What's going on!" he demanded.

Sarah and Dru sat cross-legged on the bed. He pulled a spindle-backed chair close to them and propped his feet on the table.

"I haven't seen you in several days," Sarah said. "Not since that first night in the hospital. A lot has happened!" She glanced at Brad. "After Mr. Abbott caught us in the hall, and said all those ugly things about me, I really wanted to die! It seemed like everyone I had known all my life had suddenly turned against me. I wasn't even sure my parents didn't halfway believe that the things the boys had written on the walls of our house weren't true. When I got off the bus that day, I only wanted to be alone. I watched you go inside Brannock Hall, and I knew the painters would still be working at my house.

"For some reason, I thought of the old kitchen and how quiet it always is. I cut through the yard so no one would see me, and went in. I sat there by myself for a long time. I don't know how long, but it was beginning to get dark. Somehow, I gradually began to feel better. Instead of feeling humiliated, I began to feel angry! I knew I hadn't done anything wrong. The people who were trying to hurt me were the wrong ones!

"I went home and thought about it all night, and began to form a plan." She looked at Brad and smiled. "I came to Brannock Hall the next afternoon to tell you about it. That's when I found you unconscious on the kitchen floor. I couldn't find Dru the next day, and by then everything was happening."

"What!" exclaimed Dru and Brad.

"Remember the sirens you heard last night? That was the county police. They were racing out to the migrant tenant houses. The people out there were being attacked. I made Eduardo promise that if anything ever happened he would call me. I didn't know if he really would, because his people don't have a lot of faith in us, but when he saw the cars surrounding his house, he did. When I got the call, I phoned Deputy Travers, and he sent about a dozen county police cars out there. They caught the attackers before they could hurt anybody. The gang leaders were the two boys we stopped from hurting Eduardo in the hall that day, but you'll never guess who else was in the gang!"

Brad and Dru could only look at her in surprise.

"Mr. Abbott!" They found a cross and a can of kerosene in his car. He's in jail right now, though he swears the kerosene was for his heater, and the cross for his mother's Sunday School class." She frowned in disgust.

"Did Aunt Kate go out there, too?" asked Dru in astonishment.

"Oh, yes! I called her and Mrs. Duncan, too. They've been working for weeks on a plan they're going to present to the county council which will force the farmers to provide the workers a fair wage and decent housing. It's sure to pass. Miss Kate's been doing all the legal research and Mrs. Duncan has been drumming up support. She's into just about everything in the county, and knows almost everybody. People generally do what she wants just so she'll leave them alone."

Brad sat looking at Sarah. "You did all this," he said at last. "People around here didn't care about the migrant workers until you began to fight for them."

Sarah raised her head and smiled at him with her blue eyes. Wisps of dark hair curled softly around her flushed face. For a split second Brad was startled. They had been Adalicia's eyes which smiled at him!

"They just needed to be shaken up a little," she laughed. "Now, everybody cares - Miss Kate, Ida Lou, Deputy Travers, Mr. Henderson, Mr. Anderson, my parents. Everybody!"

Brad continued to stare at her. When he spoke, his voice was unsteady. "When you went into the old kitchen that day to think, did you feel anything ... strange?"

"Strange?" Sarah whispered. She hesitated.

Dru reached out and took her hand. "It's okay," she said. "You can tell us."

"Well," Sarah's voice was low. "When I first went into the kitchen, I was so depressed that for a long time I couldn't do anything but sit and cry. But then, after a while - I don't know how long - I became aware that there was a low, humming noise in the air. I can't even be sure it was really there. I sensed it more than heard it. It also seemed as though something very, very soft was stroking my face. I wasn't at all frightened. I sat very quietly, and after a few minutes, I began to feel so much better!"

She stopped and looked at Brad and Dru.

"Go on!" Dru urged.

"You'll think I'm making this up, or that I'm crazy or something, but I gradually became aware of a great love and support in that old building. Even after it got dark and I knew Mom would be worried, I didn't want to leave. When I finally did leave, I had regained all my confidence. I knew I could fight again!"

Dru had been staring at Brad while Sarah spoke. "We have a lot to tell her," she said. "All this time we thought she was in danger from the ghost and tried to keep her away, but ever since we came to Brannock Hall, Daniel has been trying to get us to help her."

"Yes," agreed Brad. "He's been around here for one hundred and thirty years, freezing and stinking, but he never really got frantic until he realized Sarah was in trouble!"

Dru spoke thoughtfully. "Even after he finally killed LeFevre, he couldn't rest because he wanted to clear Adalicia's name. He kept trying to make contact, but all he did was scare people away until Aunt Kate moved in. That must have been really frustrating for him! She thought he was routine night noises and dead possums for thirty years. I wonder if he would have eventually just given up and faded away if he hadn't realized Sarah needed him. I don't know what would have happened if we hadn't come to Brannock Hall. He was so worried that something terrible would happen to Sarah, just like it did to Adalicia, that he was building up a dangerously angry power."

Sarah was looking at them in amazement. "Who is this Daniel?" she asked, "and why is he so worried about me? Do you mean there is actually a ghost here at Brannock Hall?" She glanced around her fearfully.

Brad grinned. He jumped off his chair. "Look," he said. "I'm starving! Why don't you two wait here? I'll bring up some doughnuts and orange juice and we can tell you all about it while we eat."

He paused at the door and looked back at

Sarah. The sun was pouring through the window, lighting the fine hairs which escaped from the pink sweatband around her head. Her legs in their spandex tights were crossed beneath her body. The headphones of her radio were looped carelessly around her neck. She caught his glance, and gave him a brilliant smile.

"A twentieth century Adalicia!" he thought. "What could be nicer?"

If you would like more information about Playground Books products, please fill out the form below and send it back to us. Thank you for your interest.

NAME _____

ADDRESS _____

CITY _____ STATE _____ ZIP _____

PHONE (HOME) _____ PHONE (WORK) _____

# OF CHILDREN IN YOUR HOME _____ THEIR AGES _____

**Playground Books Publishing Company**
**P.O. Box 3030**
**Wilmington, DE 19804**

Postage